NOBODY LIKES A FALLEN ANGEL

BOBBY TOWNSEND

NOBODY LIKES A FALLEN ANGEL

iUniverse books may be ordered through booksellers or by contacting:

iUniverse
1663 Liberty Drive
Bloomington, IN 47403
www.iuniverse.com
844-349-9409

Because of the dynamic nature of the Internet, any web addresses or links contained in this book may have changed since publication and may no longer be valid. The views expressed in this work are solely those of the author and do not necessarily reflect the views of the publisher, and the publisher hereby disclaims any responsibility for them.

Any people depicted in stock imagery provided by Getty Images are models, and such images are being used for illustrative purposes only.
Certain stock imagery © Getty Images.

ISBN: 978-1-6632-1963-3 (sc)
ISBN: 978-1-6632-1964-0 (e)

Library of Congress Control Number: 2021905695

Print information available on the last page.

iUniverse rev. date: 03/22/2021

DEDICATION

To my mom, Marjorie Groton-Townsend; my grandmother, Jessie Thayer-Groton; and my second-grade teacher, Mrs. Eleanor M. Lucier, the three ladies who inspired me to become a writer. . .

. . . And my beautiful wife, Ronni, who inspired me to continue writing.

CONTENTS

CHAPTER 1

JUST LIKE MARLENE JOBERT

The thing I remember the most is her sleek and shimmering black raincoat. She walked in with all the grace and elegance of royalty, but it wasn't the raincoat that made her look so tremendously regal. She was managing that all by herself. Her short dark hair had a sensuous flare. But all of that – the hairstyle, her raincoat and demeanor - could take a back seat to her eyes. Her eyes were bluer and more daring than the deepest blue sea. They were captivating. And, at that moment, they were cast directly on me.

I was sitting in a booth, drinking along with three more of Brockton's finest. Hell, no, I'm not talking about cops. Newspapermen. It's the men - and, of course, women – of the Fourth Estate whose constant search for facts and the reporting of them that ensure the perseverance of truth, justice and the American way. Or something like that. The four of us at the table were employees of *The Brockton Examiner,* a daily newspaper with a circulation of about 100,000 in this tired, old factory city, 20 miles south of Boston. I had been working there for seven years and was a copy editor. I also wrote a general interest column once a week on the editorial page.

Actually, now that I think about it, I'm not sure how much any of us could preserve the American way, working for a newspaper with a circulation of only a hundred thousand, but what the hell? We did our best. We were drinking at *The Ambassador,* a gin joint

1

behind the newspaper. Billy Joel was telling everyone from the juke box that John at the bar was a friend of his and gave him his drinks for free.

"*. . . And he's quick with a joke or to light up your smoke. . .*"

This was back in the days when juke boxes were common in watering holes across the country. It was 1975. Wednesday night, October 29, 1975, to be exact. Billy Joel's *Piano Man* had been released a couple of years earlier.

Heads turned when the doll I mentioned sashayed into *The Ambassador.* She removed her sparkling raincoat, draping it over the back of a barstool, and that's where her look of pure *elegance* disappeared. She was wearing a low-cut blouse, a mini skirt that was obscenely short and spiked heels. She was far and away beyond *elegant.* She sat catty-corner on the stool and her eyes immediately met mine and she held them there. She looked more like Marlene Jobert than Marlene Jobert, herself. Jobert, the actress, the drop-dead gorgeous actress.

"She's undressing you with her eyes," said John Livingston, my on-again, off-again best friend at the paper. He was sitting next to me in the booth. "Do you know her?"

"Yeah, I met her at the party after the fight."

I didn't have to specify which fight I was talking about. The one and only fight worth mentioning in Brockton at the time was an exhibition bout between Sean Casey, a former heavyweight champ of Ireland and the British Isles, and, hold onto your hats now, Yours Truly. It's a long story how that particular skirmish came to be, but that's not important right now. All you have to know is that there was this huge get-together at a function hall after the bout and that's where I met the goddess who just walked into *The Ambassador.* The goddess's son, accompanied by his mom, approached me after the fight with a poster in his hand –the photos of Sean Casey and myself adorning it – and asked me for an autograph.

"Well, don't be a fool," John urged now, "approach her."

2

"I flirted a little bit with her at the party. She put me down; she put me down hard; she's married."

Long moments passed. The doll was sipping her drink and I had about finished mine.

"She doesn't look very married to me," John said.

"Let me out of the booth," I said.

John stood and I slid across the vinyl seat and got up rather gingerly. Yeah, it had been a week since my showdown with Irish Sean Casey and my ribs were still as tender as a proverbial baby's bottom. The bout left me with three broken ribs on the left side and two on the right. I learned that when I went for x-rays the next day. The trip to the hospital was pretty much unnecessary – they don't do anything for broken ribs - but I was rewarded for my effort with a script for Oxycodone which always goes well with vodka and tonic.

I approached the young lady who was still watching me – quite expectantly now – and asked, "Can I buy you a drink?"

Yeah, great line, Rocky. Very clever; extremely original.

She smiled– a very charming, disarming smile – and nodding to the glass in front of her replied, "You just did. I told the bartender to put this one on your tab."

Yup, John at the bar was a friend of mine, but then again, he *never* gave me my drinks for free.

I looked toward the barkeep, John, and he smiled and said, "I knew you wouldn't object to buying this pretty young lady a drink."

I swallowed the rest of my vodka and tonic, put my empty glass on the bar and said, "I'll have another, John, and so will the pretty young lady."

"Do you remember me?" she asked.

"Sure, you're the kid's mother; the kid who wanted my autograph."

"*The kid* has a name. It's Bruce Archambault."

I couldn't detect if she was being a bit indignant in her reply.

"I'm sorry; I just didn't remember the youngster's name." then I asked, "Where's your husband tonight, working late again?"

The lady paused and smiled; a smile capable of lighting half of downtown Brockton on this frigid, near winter's night.

"I'm not married."

"The night of the fight you told me your husband was working late."

"No, I told you Bruce's father was working late. We're not married."

"OK, where's Bruce's father tonight, is *he* working late again?"

"I don't know. We're no longer an item. Bruce lives with his father, Arnie. Bruce had his heart set on seeing the fight and his father had to work late, so Arnie asked me to take Bruce to see it."

"Who did Bruce want to see fight, me or Irish Sean Casey?"

"Well, actually; Bruce wanted to see Sean Casey."

Another smile! Just as charming, just as disarming!

"But, you know, Bruce was very impressed when you wrote, *To Bruce, Your Pal, Rocky Scarpati*. When he got Sean Casey's autograph later that night, Casey just signed his name without writing anything. I think you won Bruce over a little bit by calling him your pal.

"Anyway, you shouldn't be upset that it wasn't *you* who he wanted to see fight. I don't think that he had ever heard of you. Quite frankly, I had never heard of Sean Casey. But I knew who you were. It was you *I wanted* to see."

"Really? Are you from around here?"

"No, I'm not from around here. I knew you from your murder trial."

I suppose that's another thing you should know about me. I once went to trial on a charge of murder. I was acquitted.

"Oh. . .that. If you're not from around here, how had you heard of my murder trial?"

"You're kidding, aren't you? Your murder trial was national news. You're famous, Well, infamous anyway."

"I'm kind of sorry that's how you came to know me," I said.

"I don't know," she allowed. "A lot of woman fall for murderers, some who are even on death row. It excites them."

4

"You excited by murderers?"

"No, I'm more excited by guys who get away with murder."

"I didn't get away with murder. I didn't do what they said I did."

"That's right, you were found not guilty. The jury said you didn't do it."

I finished my drink and motioned for John to give us a couple more. The chick with the short dark hair and brilliant eyes was drinking right along with me.

I pulled out a cigarette and put it in my mouth. That's another thing that distinguished this John from the bartender in the song. He wasn't so *quick with a joke or to light up your smoke*. I lit my own. Then as an afterthought, I held out my pack of Marlboros, offering one to the beautiful lady. She extracted one and I lit hers. The gentleman in me knew I should have offered her one first, but hey, better late than never.

"I saw you perform in *Rider on the Rain*. You were great. You were, in fact, brilliant."

She gave me the weirdest of looks.

"Didn't anyone ever tell you how much you look like Marlene Jobert?"

"Yeah, I get that a lot. But I don't see it. I don't think I look at all like her."

"Well, you do. You're her spitting image."

"I really don't think so."

"You're just being modest," I protested.

"No, I'm not being modest at all. I think I'm much better looking than Marlene Jobert."

Touché.

I asked the chick where she was from and she simply repeated, "Not around here."

"Well, if you're not from around here, what brought you to Brockton?" I asked.

"Business."

I told her I didn't think anyone did business in Brockton anymore.

I told her – maybe not for the first time – that she had very beautiful eyes.

She asked me if I wanted to leave with her.

It was just like that, right out of left field. *"Do you want to leave with me?"*

I asked her if she was a prostitute.

"Why, do I look like a prostitute?" she asked, sounding only mildly offended.

"Well, I don't know. Well, yeah, you look like a prostitute, which isn't a bad thing. I mean, the way you're dressed, very sexy, with the spiked heels and all. And a lot of makeup. Prostitutes are known to wear a lot of makeup. Yeah, you look a little bit like a prostitute. And then there was the directness of your question. Most prostitutes want to know right from the outset if you're ready to do business. They don't want to waste their time with you if you don't want to spend your money, have sex and pay for it. And if you say that's what you want, they go straight to the issue of cash, telling you what it's going to cost. I'm rambling, aren't I?"

"Yes, you're rambling and no, I'm not a hooker."

"That's good; that's very good because I don't think I could afford you if you were. I mean, you're so damn beautiful. If you were a prostitute, I'm certain you'd charge way above what I could afford."

"You certainly do know how to sweet talk a girl, don't you?"

"I really do like your spiked heels, by the way. They're very becoming."

"You still didn't answer my question," she said.

"Oh yeah, what was that?"

"Do you want to leave?"

"I want to finish my drink first," I said. "I don't have a place to bring you to. I have a live-in girlfriend who probably wouldn't appreciate your spiked heels walking into our apartment."

"That's no problem," she said. "I have a room at the *Palace Hotel.*"

"That's great," I said, "let's go."

"I thought you wanted to finish your drink first."

I picked up my drink and chugged it.

She smiled.

"Now order another one," she said. "I want to finish *my* drink."

I liked this broad's attitude. I really did; I liked it a lot.

CHAPTER 2
MEETING THE INCREDIBLE HULK

"So what's your name; I don't even know your name?" I asked.

"Eva Green."

"Hmm, it doesn't sound French. I kind of assumed you were French."

"Why, because I'm Bruce Archambault's mom?"

"Yeah, I guess so. That and because you look so much like Marlene Jobert."

"I'm Jewish."

So, yeah, I ordered another drink just as Eva had suggested and we laughed and talked and enjoyed each other's company. Then I actually ordered another round before we left for *The Palace*. It had to be around 11:30, maybe even later. Right before we left, Eva said she had to make a telephone call.

"I'm supposed to meet an old friend in a little while," she explained. "I've got to call and tell him I can't make it."

"Throwing over an old boyfriend for me?" I said, "I'm flattered."

"Don't let it go to your head; I once tossed the same guy over for a girl."

That statement certainly captured my imagination.

"Actually, it was a couple of girls," she added.

And that made my imagination run wild.

Eva scooped up some change that was in front of me and walked past the booth where my friends were sitting to a pay phone at the end of the bar. Just like the days when juke boxes were big in drinking establishments, these were also the days before everybody and his 5-year-old sister had a cell phone and pay phones were very common in all public establishments. As she passed the table where my friends were sitting, she turned heads. I figured that happened everywhere she roamed.

Eva wasn't on the telephone a minute.

"That was quick," I said when she returned.

"It doesn't take long to tell someone that you're not going to be there," she said.

I helped Eva on with her shiny, black raincoat and grabbed my blue one. My co-workers always kidded me about the raggedy, blue raincoat. But I couldn't get rid of it even if I wanted to. It would tarnish my image. I was well known for my *Famous Blue Raincoat*.

It was only a short walk from *The Ambassador* to *The Palace*, which was a good thing because, baby, it was getting cold outside. Neither one of our coats was heavy enough for the weather. When Eva mentioned how frigid it was, I put my arm around her and that's how we walked to *The Palace*. Her spiked heels made her just about my height. It was sort of misty earlier in the evening and, with the cold weather, the sidewalks were slippery. Eva stumbled along in her spiked heels, being careful not to slip and fall; and I kept my arm around her, attempting to keep both of us upright. Of course, by now I had had several drinks and, although I handled my liquor extremely well, I was a bit unsteady on my feet. We joked and stumbled and laughed and it was a very pleasant walk, indeed.

The Palace, contrary to its name, was an old, red brick building. Not very large – I mean, for a hotel and certainly not for a palace - and not impressive at all. We crossed a small parking lot behind the hotel to get to the back door. There was a dirty old pickup truck, a beat-up old Ford Fairlane 500 that looked a lot like my first car, a little green car that probably came off the assembly line during the

Eisenhower administration, a blue VW with a flat tire and a sleek, shiny black Lincoln. The Lincoln looked out of place.

We walked through the back door and past a lounge to the elevator. I drank at *The Palace* more than occasionally and I hoped I'd see some of the people I knew at the lounge. Eva was definitely a trophy and it would be cool to have people see us together. *See us going up in an elevator together; to a room; my arm around her.* There were very few people in the lounge, though, and I don't think any of them paid us any notice.

Eva inserted the key into the door, turned it, swung the door open and stepped aside for me to enter. I took a step inside - and was hammered by a goon the size of *The Incredible Hulk*. Of course, that's my description now. It wasn't a comparison I made then. It would be a few years before *The Hulk* made his television debut.

I was slammed in the side! I crashed to the floor! I looked up and saw Eva close the door. Lock it. My eyes teared, which embarrassed the hell out of me. Tough guys don't cry. But the pain was excruciating. I couldn't catch my breath. Maybe it wouldn't have been so bad if my ribs hadn't been shattered previously. I felt like vomiting. I looked up and saw *The Hulk* slip brass knuckles off his right hand and put them into his suit jacket pocket. He was wearing a pin-striped suit with a white shirt. No tie, though! But shit, a pin-striped suit! He didn't have to dress on my account.

I looked up at this dude from the floor and it felt kind of like being in New York City and looking up at the Empire State Building. Have you ever been in New York City, staring up at the Empire State Building? It's so tall you feel like you're getting dizzy just looking up at it. That's the way it felt when I was looking up. I was getting dizzy looking at him. Of course, my crash to the floor might have had something to do that.

The dude was an ugly son-of-a-bitch. He had a flat face and a wide nose that looked like it might have been splattered and very thick eyebrows that were broken up in several places by scar tissue. The scar tissue was heavy around both eyes. He looked like he probably had been a prize fighter, himself, at one time or another - a heavyweight, obviously. He was about 6-5 and on the northern side of 250 pounds. As big and as heavy as he was, he wasn't fat. He was broad shouldered, barrel-chested; had muscled arms. He kept himself in good shape.

The Hulk handed Eva a pair of handcuffs and said: "Cuff him, hands in the front of him."

Eva knelt in front of me and leaned forward to cuff my hands. You know, with her blouse cut so low to begin with and her leaning forward like that, I got the most glorious bird's eye view of a couple of the most glamorous breasts this side of the Playboy Mansion. It made me regret the terrible turn of events and what the hell was I thinking about anyway? Here I am laying on the floor of a hotel room with *The Hulk* standing over me and feeling like I got red-hot pokers in my side and I'm worried about the sex I'm missing with the angel in front of me, the angel who's a devil in disguise. Then the strangest thing happened – and you're probably not going to believe this, but it happened - as Eva was putting the handcuffs on me - she mouthed the words, "I'm sorry."

Of course, her being sorry and a quarter wouldn't buy me a cup of coffee anymore.

"Stand up!" *The Hulk* demanded. His voice was like a drill sergeant.

When I didn't move fast enough, *The Hulk* kicked me. It wasn't very hard. It wasn't like he was trying to boot a 50-yard field goal or anything. I'm sure it was just a chip shot – an extra point conversion - from *The Hulk's* point of view. But it got the message across and I got to my feet as fast as my broken ribs would allow.

"Eva, on the couch, my overcoat," *The Hulk* said. I guess that was his way of telling her to fetch it.

She handed it to him and he draped the coat over my hands in front of me, hiding the handcuffs.

"We're gonna walk out of here," he said as he reached under the back of his own suit jacket and pulled out a pistol that had been tucked in his pants. Then he pulled a silencer out of his suit jacket pocket and attached it.

"We're gonna walk out of here and you're not gonna say a fuckin' word. If you do, I swear on my mother's grave, I'll shoot you right here in the hotel."

"I'll bet your mother ain't even dead," I said.

The Hulk opened his mouth as if he was going to respond, but then he hesitated, considering what he was going to say. He didn't think of anything, closed his mouth again and didn't say a damn thing. He draped his overcoat over the gun and motioned for me to leave the room.

"You know, nobody's gonna fall for this," I said. "It's goddamn cold outside. Everybody's gonna wonder why you're not wearing your coat and then they're going to say, 'Of course, he's not wearing a coat because he's hiding a gun under it.'"

The Hulk opened his mouth again, thought about a comeback and couldn't figure one out. So he just said, "Shut the fuck up!"

When we walked by the lounge, the same few people who didn't pay attention to us before unfortunately didn't pay attention to us again.

We walked out the same back door Eva and I had entered and straight to the shiny black Lincoln. *The Hulk* put me in the back seat. Not too gracefully. He put tape over my mouth. Then he took a length of cloth and tied it around my head, eye level, blindfolding me. Then, on top of all that, he put a hood over my head. He told Eva to sit in back with me. Then I felt her beside me, her arm and leg against mine. There was plenty of room in the back seat. I was against the passenger-side rear door. And Eva was against me like there were three people sitting back there. What was all that about?

As we were pulling out, I got to thinking - not for the first time - that *The Incredible Hulk* wasn't too bright. He's got me sitting in the backseat in a hood. Someone will see me, know something is wrong and call the cops.

Then it hit me. I remembered the Lincoln - or whatever it was - in the parking lot had tinted windows. They were very heavily tinted. Nobody would see me sitting inside.

The excursion was stop and go at the outset. We were obviously heading out of downtown Brockton where the traffic lights were numerous and very poorly timed. After five – 10 or 12? – minutes we were traveling right along and obviously on a highway so, using my acute powers of deduction, I knew we were on Route 24. We veered to the right and then made a wide, swooping left turn so I figured we were on Route 95. When we were a few minutes onto 95, I felt Eva's hand on my thigh, very high on my thigh. She massaged it slowly. I got an erection. Can you believe that? I'm in the backseat of a shiny black Lincoln, getting kidnapped and I'm getting an erection? Well, Eva was the kind of a chick who could make that happen. Her hand stayed there on my thigh for about a minute before she gave my leg a final little squeeze and let go. A minute may not seem like a very long time, but if you've ever been blindfolded and gagged in the back seat of a Lincoln and the sexiest chick this side of the Cape Cod Canal ever put her hand on your thigh and held it there for a minute, then you know it's a very long time.

We left the highway and made a right turn, then a left and then another right. Or was it a left turn, then a right and then another left? You'd think I would have done a better job of memorizing the route, wouldn't you? You know, just in case I needed to describe it to investigators sometime in the future. I just know we made three turns and then the automobile slowed down. And Eva took my hand in hers and gave it a reassuring squeeze. It didn't reassure me at all.

CHAPTER 3

DON'T PAY THE RANDSOM, HONEY...

It was well after midnight when we slowed down, made a sharp right turn and the Lincoln came to a stop. I figured we were in a driveway. I sensed Eva leaving my side and sliding over to the seat behind the driver. Then I heard both *The Hulk* and Eva step out of the car. My door opened and *The Hulk* ordered me to get out. I started out reluctantly and *The Hulk* grabbed my arm and pulled me forward in a hurry. He closed the car door behind me and again yanked me forward. He rapped on a door and a voice told us to come in. It was a gravelly, hoarse, harsh voice. One I thought I knew. One I feared I knew.

The Hulk sat me down in a chair.

"Take off the hood," the voice ordered.

The Hulk tugged it from my head.

Then, "Take off the blindfold."

Yup, it was the face I anticipated seeing. Angel. I was looking into his dark, bulging eyes. Cold, cold as a witch's tit. And the vicious scar under his right eye.

I think right about now is a good time to tell you a little bit about the murder rap that resulted in my trial. I didn't beat and kill Lou Montgomery in a Providence, R.I., parking garage as the authorities were alleging. Angel did. But I was just as guilty as Angel. Maybe more so. I had hired him.

It's like this: My international union, the Amalgamated Media Guild, was on strike against *The Providence Chronicle*. This dude, Lou Montgomery, was the head of the National Crafts Union in Providence and the NCU was breaking our picket line daily, going into work, setting type and putting out a newspaper. And then our international representative, who was leading the Guild strike, was beaten and put in a hospital. We were certain Montgomery and his union were responsible and our international president wanted revenge. I was a union activist and had a friend with underworld ties so I hired Angel, a Providence "hit man" to do the job. Montgomery wasn't supposed to be killed, only put into the hospital. But when Angel slugged the dude, Montgomery went down, struck his head and met his maker.

I wrestled with my conscience. Particularly when I learned that the victim was a family man, a Boy Scout leader and a Little League baseball coach. But I kept telling myself he was a strikebreaker, also known far and wide in union circles as a scab. And any union leader worth his membership card will tell you that a scab is the lowest form of life. I kept telling myself that. I just wasn't certain if I totally believed it.

When authorities investigated the murder, I had the motive. Well, that being said, of course I did, but so did a shitload of other union members. But I soon learned much to my complete and utter dismay that there was all kinds of circumstantial evidence that suggested I was the person who slugged Montgomery on that fateful day. My trial was a roller coaster ride. There were times I felt doomed. In the end, though, after several days of deliberation, a jury found me not guilty. So, now here I was face to face with the man who had actually struck and killed the *scab* who led his union through our picket line. And I had a pretty good idea what the subject matter of this meeting was going to be about. I was pretty shook up. But I wasn't going to give Angel the satisfaction of showing it.

"Angel," I said, "it's good to see you."

He was wearing a very powerful, distinctive cologne. Wearing too much of it. I kind of remembered that about him the first time I met him. I didn't pay as much attention to it back then, though. We were outdoors when I met him. The smell wasn't as overwhelming. But here it was strong enough to gag a maggot.

Now we were in a tiny bungalow. Not much more than a shack actually, a box. We were sitting at a sticky Formica table in a 2x4 kitchen. There was an old stove and refrigerator, a loaf of bread and a toaster on a greasy countertop, some cooking utensils hanging from the wall and bottles of booze strewn here, there and everywhere. Angel didn't offer me a drink.

Beyond the kitchen was a living room with a sofa and a tremendously worn recliner, its stuffing protruding from the arms. I noticed a totally non-descript waterfront picture on one wall and a snow-capped mountain on another, the kind of boring stuff you'd see hanging in a dentist's waiting room. A bedroom – its walls bare – was beyond the living room and a small bathroom was off the bedroom.

"Nice place you've got here," I said.

He grunted.

Angel motioned to a small refrigerator and said, "Eva, get me an apple." His voice was gravel. As pleasant as a metal fork caught in a garbage disposal. Eva fetched the apple and handed it to Angel. He produced a very large switchblade, the size of a small sword, and snapped it open. He extracted a slice from the apple and shoved it in his mouth. He chewed it without closing his mouth. I was certain the whole procedure was meant to intimidate me and he certainly accomplished that, but I didn't let it show. At least, I don't think I did.

"I'm kind of surprised you sent King Kong here to retrieve me," I said. "I thought you were the strong-arm. I didn't know you had to resort to hiring *stronger arms* to do *your* dirty work."

"I couldn't risk being seen with you," he responded. "There can't be no connection between you and me."

"Well, you didn't have to send King Kong and Fay Wray to bring me here. All you had to do was give me a call and I'd have been happy to meet you at the dog track just like old times." I was doing my best to sound like a bad ass myself.

"This ain't like no old times," Angel growled back. "We can't be seen together at no dog track or any other fuckin' place." Then he repeated. "It's very important we don't be seen together. I was arrested for the murder of that guy from *The Chronicle*, ahhh, what's his name?"

"Lou Montgomery," I reminded him.

"Yeah, Lou Montgomery."

"Johnny McCracken told me."

Angel's bulging eyes somehow managed to widen.

"Who's Johnny McCracken?"

"He's a Brockton detective. He asked me if I knew you. Scared me shitless that he had figured out the connection between you, me and Lou Montgomery. I thought he had caught on to the fact that I hired you to beat the shit outta Montgomery."

"Did he? Did he figure it out?"

There was a real sense of urgency in Angel's voice now.

"No, he just wanted to know if I knew you or had heard of you. You know, because you were charged with the same murder I went to trial for? He said he wanted me to know the Providence cops finally got the right guy."

He shoved another slice of apple into his mouth. Again, he chewed it with his mouth open.

"You're gonna tell them they didn't get the right guy." Angel didn't just say it. He spat out the words along with a couple of tiny pieces of apple that sprayed onto the table.

When I didn't respond, he added: "You already went to trial for the murder of Montgomery. They can't charge you with it again. It would be ah... ah... whatta ya call it? Double jeopardies. So you can turn around now and tell them you actually did it. They can't touch you."

"I can't do that!"

All kinds of reasons swarmed through my head. How the hell would it affect my daughter when she got old enough to understand? How would it affect my job? Could I be fired for being a murderer? And my reputation, what about my reputation? Although my reputation had already taken a pretty good hit. Being found not guilty of a crime doesn't necessarily mean you didn't do it. Particularly when you didn't testify at your trial and tell the world you didn't do it. People wonder about that. I'm sure there were plenty of people out there who were pretty well convinced that I had offed Lou Montgomery.

So, anyway, I told Angel I couldn't do that and he told me he wasn't asking me; he was telling me. Then he put out his hand and, as if on cue, King Kong handed him a stack of 8x10 black and white pictures. Angel flipped them down on the table in front of me one at a time. There was a photo of my ex-wife, Susan, walking with our beautiful daughter, Jennifer Ann, who was almost two years old now. I always called her Annie. I know I was a rotten father. Rotten for leaving. But I loved Annie. I paid child support regularly and took her out all the time. She was my life. I know you're not going to believe that. I know you're going to say I had a funny way of showing it. . . Yeah, I did.

There was another picture of my little girl playing in one of those little inflatable swimming pools in the backyard of my ex's apartment. So Angel knew where Susan lived. There was one of Susan standing next to Annie, who was on a merry-go-round. It looked like it was in some sort of shopping mall. And then Angel placed a picture of Barbara, my live-in girlfriend, in front of me. It was taken outside our apartment building so I guess that was to show me he knew where we lived, too.

"You wouldn't want anything to happen to any – or all – of your loved ones," Angel said.

I wanted to tell him to fuck off and go to hell. I wanted to tell him if anything happened to my loved ones, I'd see him dead before he got to trial. But that just didn't seem like the appropriate attitude to take at the moment. It seemed like Angel was holding all the high cards and I was sitting there with a pair of deuces.

"You don't need me to confess," I said instead. "Get the same attorney I had defending me, Frank Agnesi. He's right here in Providence. He's great. He'll get you off, no sweat. Particularly when the cops were already convinced I did it."

"Frank Agnesi *is* my lawyer! But he can't handle this rap for me 'cuz he already handled *this* murder for you. He said something about he couldn't be interested in my case 'cuz it would be conflicting his interests. So you screwed me there, too, Scarpati. You took my lawyer.

"So I want to know right now, Scarpati. Are you gonna confess to the cops you did it? If not, maybe me and my friend here can do some convincin' right now!"

Time. I needed time to think. But I knew I wasn't going to get any if I said that to Angel.

"Yeah, I'll tell them I did it."

After I told Angel that I'd confess to the murder, *The Hulk* was instructed to drive me back to where he got me. They put the blindfold and the hood back on. I asked Angel why that was necessary and he growled, "Ain't that fuckin' obvious? We don't want you to know where we are!" At least, this time, they didn't find it necessary to put my hands in cuffs. *The Hulk* drove me back to *The Ambassador* in Brockton and dropped me off. It was about a half-hour trip, the same as it was when we going in the opposite direction. After the blindfold was removed, I noticed that *The Hulk* still had on those goddamn thin black gloves. I walked to my car, which was in a lot near *The Examiner*. It must have been about 2:30 before I got home.

I walked into our apartment and there was Guido, Barbara's son. Guido was 14 at the time. He was sitting in the living room eating Cheetos and watching television. The volume was turned down really low, I suppose in deference to his mother's sleeping in a room down the hall.

"What are you doing up so late on a school night?" I asked.

"Eating Cheetos"

Not exactly what I was looking for, but I guess that covered it.

Barbara woke up when I walked into the bedroom and asked groggily, "Where you been?"

"I was kidnapped."

"That's an old joke. *'Don't pay the ransom, honey, I escaped.'*"

"Yeah, I know. Except I'm not joking."

She rubbed the sleep from her eyes and wearily asked, "What happened?"

I told her about the events of the evening, leaving out, of course, about being lured to the *Palace Hotel* by the more-than-lovely Eva Green. I told her that *The Hulk* appeared from an alley when I left *The Ambassador* by its rear door and he blasted me with brass knuckles into my already broken hips. Then he produced the gun and ordered me into the shiny black limo. When I told Barbara about meeting Angel, believe it or not, it was the first time I had ever told her the whole story surrounding the death of Lou Montgomery.

While I talked, Barbara, in all her radiant, naked glory, rolled a joint, took a couple of tokes and handed it to me.

"Here, this should help you deal with those busted ribs," she said, as always, talking out of the side of her mouth. That was one of the things I loved about Barbara; she always talked out of the side of her mouth. Made her sound like she had a chip on her shoulder. A tough broad. Which she was. She wasn't your typical American female beauty. She was short with olive skin and short, frosted hair and firm breasts. A very prominent chin. But she had an ass and legs that were out of this world, which made her very attractive to me. And other men.

Barbara leaned over and kissed me tenderly when I had finished my saga.

CHAPTER 4

PARTIAL ECLIPSE OF THE SUN

I don't know how I managed to do it, but I went to work a few hours later that morning. After work, I walked out of the front door of *The Examiner* into a partial eclipse of the sun. There he was, *The Incredible Hulk,* leaning against the big, black Lincoln that was illegally parked on Main Street in front of *The Examiner. The Hulk,* even with all his height and his girth, wasn't large enough to create a total solar eclipse, but he cast a pretty good-sized shadow.

"I'm not going for a ride," I said as I approached.

"I ain't telling you to. Where the hell you been?"

"What do you mean, *'Where the hell have I been?'* I've been working."

"I've been waiting for you!"

I wasn't sure how to respond to that. I felt like he was complaining that I was late for an appointment.

The Hulk was wearing the same pin-striped suit as he was the night before. I could tell because the same button was missing with the same thread hanging as the one last night. His white shirt was a different one, though. A mustard stain I had spotted the night before wasn't there.

"You ain't confessed to the murder yet, have you?" *The Hulk* asked. "You ain't told the cops you did it?"

So that's what this visit was about!

"No, I told Angel I'd tell the cops I did it. I didn't say I'd tell them today."

"That's OK, Angel don't want you to."

Suddenly, I felt a wave of relief. But it was just as suddenly snatched away.

"Angel, he told me to tell you he don't want you talkin' to no cops right now. He had a conversation with his lawyer about it and his lawyer wants you to wait until the trial. They're gonna call you as a witness and that's when you're gonna say you done it."

"Oh, yeah … That's … when I'll say I did it."

There were a couple moments of silence.

"Who's Angel's lawyer, anyhow?" I asked. Not that the name would mean anything to me. I didn't know any lawyers in Rhode Island except good old Frank Agnesi and we had already established that Angel couldn't be using Frank.

"Tommy Tomaselli," *Hulk* said. Just as I thought; the name didn't mean a thing to me.

"You know, Angel's really bullshit at you for using Frank Agnesi," *Hulk* said.

"Yeah, he got that point across."

"I heard you used to be a fighter," *Hulk* said.

This was getting really strange, *The Hulk* and I chit-chatting outside *The Examiner* like a couple of old friends. What was I supposed to do, invite him to *The Ambassador* for a drink?

"You any relation to Rocky Marciano?"

The question threw me for a loop.

"Of course not," I said. "His last name was Marciano, mine's Scarpati."

"Well, I just thought you were both fighters and you were both from Brockton and Italian and everything and there are a lot of very big Italian families; I thought you might be related. Besides," *Hulk* added, "you're both named Rocky."

Not the first time I thought that this very large dude was no mental giant.

I had intended to go straight home after work, I really had. I mean, I was extremely weary after my escapade the night before. But, after my meeting with *The Incredible Hulk,* I needed a drink. So I turned the corner at the front of *The Examiner* and walked down the alleyway to *The Ambassador.* Unusual, I didn't see any *Examiner* people there yet, but that was fine with me. I wanted to be alone. I needed to think. I was sitting at the bar when Henry Nickalou walked in. Henry was a friend of mine and a lawyer in Brockton. He recommended Frank Agnesi to represent me in Rhode Island. He was also one of the very few people I told that I didn't do it. I told him I wasn't the dude who beat the shit out of Lou Montgomery in the Providence parking garage. Although I never told Henry that I had hired Angel, the dude who did.

Henry, a bulky, sort of unkempt dude with short, wiry hair and smoking a pipe reminiscent of Sherlock Holmes's, came into *The Ambassador* with a small group of guys – I recognized them all as attorneys – but when he saw me, he excused himself and joined me at the bar. John, the barkeep, wondered over and Henry ordered a Miller Lite and whatever I was drinking, which was a vodka and tonic.

"What are you doing sitting here all alone?" Henry asked.

"I wanted to be alone; I've got to think," I responded, but quickly added, "but wait, stay, you're just the person I need to talk to."

"What's wrong?" Henry asked.

"Did you see they made another arrest in the murder of Lou Montgomery?" I asked. "They arrested some dude out of Providence."

"Yeah, I saw an article about it in *The Globe* and that was a major topic of conversation at the courthouse. I guess that just goes to show the jury in your case got it right. Anthony Fazio (the district attorney) must now be convinced that you actually were not guilty and that this other guy -what's his name? – was."

I filled in the blank, "Angelo Macrillo. They call him Angel, but his name is Angelo Macrillo. Johnny McCracken told me he's also known as *Mac the Knife* because of his weapon of choice. Angel carries a switchblade with him and he's been known to slice and dice anyone who crosses him."

"Well, Fazio must be convinced this Angel or *Mac the Knife* or whatever you want to call him did the dirty deed if Fazio is taking him to trial."

One, two, three beats of silence and then Henry asked, "Is that what's bothering you, the fact that another arrest was made?"

When I didn't answer right away, Henry added, "Why?"

Two men in business suits had just sat down on the stools to my left, so I motioned to an empty booth and asked Henry if we could sit there. I didn't want to be overheard. He said sure.

"Believe it or not, I was kidnapped last night (Henry's eyes widened in amazement) and was taken to see Angel."

"Who kidnapped you?"

I told him how the most beautiful chick in the world picked me up at *The Ambassador* and brought me back to the *Palace Hotel* where I was smashed in the side by a trained gorilla wearing brass knuckles. I told him the whole story from the night before: the blind-folded ride, the pictures, the threats; the whole shebang.

"Have you gone to the cops about it?"

"No."

"Why not?"

"Because I don't want them looking into my past dealings with this dude."

"Oh, you have a history with Angel?"

"Yup, he's a business acquaintance."

Henry gave me a nod as if to say he kind of understood. He had gotten enough of the picture to know that he didn't want to hear the full picture.

"So it looks like I might have to tell the authorities I offed Lou Montgomery to prevent serious harm from coming to the people closest to me."

"Your problem is a lot greater than you realize," Henry told me. "When this Angel character told you that you couldn't be charged with the murder because it would constitute double jeopardy, he was wrong."

Now it was my turn to look at Henry in amazement. I was fairly well acquainted with the concept of double jeopardy.

"If you had just murdered this Montgomery feller in Providence, Rhode Island," Henry said, "you would have had to cross state lines to do it. That makes it a federal offense. You were tried in a state court and found not guilty of a state charge. The feds can still charge you with murder and take you to trial. And, if you now admit to killing Montgomery, I expect that's exactly what they will do."

CHAPTER 5

NOBODY LIKES A FALLEN ANGEL

I have to admit I was a little bit relieved to know that Angel and *The Incredible Hulk* wouldn't be breathing down my back day after day, asking if I had confessed to the murder of Lou Montgomery. But, on the other hand, I felt like I was in a guillotine waiting for the blade to drop. I almost wanted it to happen just to get it over with.

I walked into *The Ambassador* three and a half weeks later and saw a familiar figure sitting at the bar. She was wearing dark glasses even in the darkened lounge. There were several *Examiner* people in *The Ambassador* that afternoon – six were sitting in a booth and a small table was pulled up to it to accommodate a couple more – but I didn't join them. I walked straight to Eva. Her right arm was in a cast.

There was Christmas music playing on the jukebox. Some chick was *Rockin' Around the Christmas Tree*. Brenda Lee? Maybe. This was a Tuesday, two days before Thanksgiving and they were already playing Christmas music on the juke box. It certainly wasn't my quarters that paid for it.

"We have to stop meeting like this," I said as I approached.

Up close, I spotted a split lip and bruises protruding from under her shades.

"Who's that person you said I was?" she asked.

The question dumbfounded me.

"What are you talking about?"

"When Maurice and I brought you to see Angel, you told him he didn't have to send King Kong and some woman to get you."

"Oh, yeah, I told him he didn't have to send King Kong and Fay Wray."

"Yeah, that's who it was, Fay Wray. Who is Fay Wray anyhow?"

John approached us and put a vodka and tonic in front of me. I told him to give Eva another drink. I noticed some discoloration extending beyond Eva's dark glasses on the left side.

"What happened to you?" I asked.

"First you answer me. Who's that woman? What's her name?"

"Fay Wray."

"Yes, who's Fay Wray?"

"She was a very beautiful actress."

"Really?" she said with a broad smile. I thought her eyes might be smiling, too, if I could have seen them under those dark glasses.

"Yeah, really."

"I thought you were making fun of me the way you were making fun of Maurice. You know, calling him King Kong."

So now I knew *The Incredible Hulk's* name. It was Maurice. He certainly didn't look like a Maurice.

"No, I wasn't making fun of you. Fay Wray was the actress the gorilla carried to the top of the Empire State Building. The very beautiful actress."

"I'm glad. It bothered me, you making fun of me."

"What happened to you?"

"Angel beat the shit out of me."

"Why?"

"I looked at some guy the wrong way. And when Angel started yelling at me about it, I made a very big mistake. I told him he didn't own me. I thought he was going to kill me this time!"

"*This time*? You mean it's happened before?"

"Yeah, but never like this. This time was the worst. If Maurice hadn't been there to stop him, I think he *would have* killed me.

Angel said he was sorry. Angel always says he's sorry and it won't happen again."

"King Kong stopped him?"

"Yeah, he watched for a little bit. When it got too violent, Maurice pulled Angel away."

"Good ape," I said, proud of my response. I thought it was clever. Then, as an afterthought I added, "Why don't you leave Angel?"

"Nobody leaves Angel, not unless they're told to."

"Have you ever tried?"

Eva shook her head slightly.

"Then how do you know you couldn't."

"He once told me if I ever left him, he'd hunt me down and make me sorry I was ever born. I believed him. He says he loves me. He just has a funny way of showing it."

"Take off the shades."

Eva glanced around the room to see if anyone was looking. But then she shrugged her shoulders like it really didn't matter and she took off her dark glasses. Both eyes were terribly blackened. Swollen. No more than slits actually. Badly bruised.

"The guy's an animal," I said.

I reached forward, cupped my hand behind her head and nudged her head toward me. I placed my lips against her left eye very gently, very gingerly, and kissed it.

When I withdrew my head, Eva looked through me.

"He bruised my lips, too," she said with a bit of a grin.

I leaned forward and placed my lips against hers. Even more tenderly than I had against her eye. Barely touching, we kissed. As I withdrew my head, it was Eva's turn to cup her hand behind it and she guided me forward again. She placed her lips against mine. Slightly firmer than before, and slipped her tongue into my mouth. Our tongues did a little dance.

"Hey, Scarpati, get a room," Bob Sinclair chided from a booth.

"That might not be a bad idea," I said to Eva.

She put the dark glasses back on.

31

"I know a place where we can go," she said.

"You're not going to tell me you've got another room at *The Palace*, are you?"

"No, but I need a ride. I haven't been driving since, you know, the broken arm."

"Where to?"

"Pawtucket."

Pawtucket, Rhode Island, was right over the line from Massachusetts, about a 20-mile ride from Brockton.

"How did you get here?" I asked.

"I got a ride with a friend who was going to Boston. It wasn't far out of her way."

"What were you going to do if I didn't stop in for a drink today?"

"I was told you stop in for a drink every day."

"Who told you that?"

"I don't know. It must have been Angel. He's made a point of learning everything about you."

"I'm flattered. You don't have anyone waiting at your place with brass knuckles, do you?"

"No, I promise."

Being the gentleman that I am, I opened the passenger-side door of my Karmen Ghia for her. I purchased the Karmen Ghia when I first got the job at *The Examiner*. Now it was seven years old. . . seven years old and dirty. It was so un-sporty, it didn't even have bucket seats in front. It had that old-fashioned bench seat, which I appreciated in a hurry when I walked around and got in the driver's side and discovered Eva had moved to the center, right by my side. By the time I pulled out of the Ward Street parking lot, she had placed her dark glasses on the dashboard and her hand was on my thigh. Very high on my thigh. By the time we turned off Ward Street, her hand had moved up onto my crotch, sending shivers all through me. On Pleasant Street she unfastened my belt.

"How are you doing that with your left hand?" I asked.

Remember, her right arm was in a cast.

"I guess I'm just lucky," she said. "I'm left-handed."

She still fumbled unfastening my pants, though, so I lent her a hand while I kept the other one on the wheel. She unzipped my pants. She pulled my boxers over my erection. We were stopped at a traffic light and there was a dude in a truck next to us, looking down into our car. He was thoroughly entertained.

"We've got a spectator," I told Eva.

She looked up. Smiled. She gave the driver a little wave.

He smiled and gave her a *thumbs up* in return.

Afterwards, we rode in silence for a little bit.

"You know what would solve our problem?" Eva said.

"What problem?" I asked. "I didn't know we had a problem."

"Angel, he's a problem for both of us."

"I guess you got that right."

"You know what would solve the problem for both of us?"

She didn't wait for me to respond.

"If Angel was dead."

"Hmmm. I guess you're right about that, too."

Silence for a while.

Then, "I got you a gun," Eva said. "I could also arrange a meeting with just you and Angel, no one to see; no one to know."

"No way in hell!"

"Why not?"

"Because I'm not a murderer!"

"So a jury said."

"I told you, I didn't do it. In fact, *you know* I didn't do it,"

More silence.

"What's this all about, some kind of little code of ethics of yours?" she asked.

"What? That I don't kill people?"

"Nobody could blame you. It would be like justifiable ah; ah what do you call it?"

"Homicide," I filled in the blank. "Justifiable homicide."

"Yeah, justifiable homicide. He threatened your girlfriend and your ex-wife and your daughter. You'd just be protecting them."

One, two, three beats.

"And you'd be protecting me," Eva added. "He'll end up killing me."

"Is that what that blow job was about back there? Payment for services you expected would soon be rendered."

"Of course not. I told you before, I ain't no hooker. I did that because . . . because I wanted to."

Quiet again.

There was a dude in a giant monster SUV riding my ass with his high-beams on. I pulled over to the travel lane and let him pass.

"If you think it's so goddamn justifiable, why don't you shoot Angel?"

"Because I could never get away with it. When someone is murdered, the first person the cops look at is the husband or wife or the girlfriend or boyfriend. As soon as they found Angel's body, the cops would be right after me."

I turned on the radio, flipped through a few stations until I found one that came in without a lot of static. Old Freddy Fender was singing about *Wasted Days and Wasted Nights*.

"You could shoot Angel and then we call the cops and report it," Eva said. "I tell them Angel was beating the shit out of me and you were saving my ass. He woulda killed me." Jesus, she just wouldn't give it up. She wouldn't take no for an answer.

"Then the cops would assume we were in it together. You said it yourself; the first one the cops look at is the girlfriend. They'd say we're lovers, we were in it together and we'd both take the fall."

"You know what? I bet we wouldn't. I bet the cops wouldn't look very hard to find Angel's killer. They'd think somebody did them a favor. They've tried to pin murders on Angel before. They'd like nothing more than to stick a needle in his arm."

"Rhode Island doesn't have the death penalty," I said.

"You know what I mean. The cops would just as soon see Angel dead."

I smiled.

"So that's what you're telling me? Nobody gives a damn about a fallen Angel, is that it? Not even the cops?"

"Exactly. Nobody likes him."

"Or you shoot him and we don't report it," Eva said. "If they ever come after you for it, I give you an alibi. I tell them you were with me."

"Same thing; that makes us co-conspirators. They look to the girlfriend like you said and she says she was with me. Then they've even got a love triangle. Gives me the oldest motive in the world. Again, we go down. No more scenarios. I'm not doing it. Period."

As Eva directed me off the highway, Helen Reddy came on the radio and told me that's *"No Way to Treat a Lady."*

Hmm, I thought, Helen got that right.

Minutes after we left the highway, we traveled along a narrow, roughly paved road. Most of the houses on it, all of which backed up to the woods, were ranch-style homes and they were pretty few and far between. The shortest distance between any two of them was probably about three football fields. After we passed four or five, Eva told me to pull into the drive of the next one. It was an extremely small bungalow, not much more than a shack actually. It wasn't much more than a box.

Eva invited me in for a nightcap.

CHAPTER 6

FISHING BOATS AND SNOW-CAPPED MOUNTAINS

Going in for the nightcap was a mistake – the biggest mistake of my life. Well, maybe not the biggest of my life. I've made some humdingers!

The tiny place looked eerily familiar. I gazed beyond the kitchen to the living room and my suspicion was immediately confirmed. A very boring painting of a harbor with fishing boats hanging on one wall and snow-capped mountains on another.

I asked, "You live here?"

"No."

"Who lives here, Angel?"

"Nobody."

"I didn't think so."

"It's just a place Angel, Maurice and I use whenever we have a reason."

"Like kidnapping and intimidating me?"

"Yeah, like that. You know I wish that never happened."

"What are we doing here now - tonight?"

"We came in for a nightcap, remember?"

She opened her handbag and pulled out a canon.

"This is the gun I got for you. If you ever change your mind, it will be here for you. Just ask for it."

Actually, it wasn't even a particularly large handgun. But, from my perspective, it *looked like* a canon.

"It's loaded," she said.

I'm not sure why she felt the need to tell me that. I didn't have any intention of touching it, much less shooting it.

She walked into the bedroom, opened the top drawer of a night table and placed the gun inside.

"I'm putting it in here."

Again, I didn't see the need to tell me.

"I won't change my mind," I assured her.

"I know you won't." She flashed the faintest of smiles.

She mixed me a vodka and tonic. Very heavy on the vodka. Besides the bottles of booze on the kitchen counter, there were some on a table in the living room and more here and there in the bedroom. She poured herself a whiskey with a splash of something or other.

Then she went to the telephone and dialed a number. She hung up without uttering a word.

"Nobody home?" I asked.

"Something like that," she responded.

Shortly afterward, we were on the bed, our drinks on the night tables beside us.

I undressed her.

Slowly.

If this were a movie, there'd be some very suspenseful music playing quietly right now, but it would be building, preparing the viewer for the trauma that was about to unfold. Of course, like any good protagonist, I would have been oblivious to it. I hadn't been as excited by the anticipation of sex since the brutally cold night I stumbled toward *The Palace Hotel* with my arm around the very same goddess I was lusting over at that very moment. Anticipation can be a killer.

Maestro, bring the music to a crescendo!

The kitchen door flew open and Angel entered. He hesitated very briefly to register what it was he was actually seeing – he probably didn't believe his bulging eyes - hollered, "BITCH!" in his grueling, gruff voice and, lumbering forward, produced his renowned switchblade, snapping it open en route. I leaped from the bed and positioned myself between Angel and the beautiful goddess. She darted into the bathroom. By now, the music would be absolutely blaring! I swear, and this will be nearly impossible for you to believe because there was, after all, no music at all, but it blared in my head! It heard it! It engulfed my senses! Every fabric of my being screeched with fear, dread and yeah -mezzo forte - the outrageously loud music. I tried to explain it several times afterwards, I couldn't. I couldn't explain what I was hearing. Not to others; not even to myself.

Angel huffed and puffed and approached like a train and I jumped in front of him in all my naked glory with my fists clenched. I had fought several dudes in the ring who had fast hands, but none as incredibly swift as Angel's, despite his bulk. He flicked a left hand in my direction. It wasn't a punch or a push or even a poke, merely a flash that captured my attention for an instant and then he swiped with his knife hand, the right, with the speed of a lightning bolt and opened a small gash in my stomach.

Inexplicably, I dropped to the floor. That's another thing I've tried and tried to fathom, but I've never been able to explain to my own satisfaction. Why did I drop to the floor? I wasn't in excruciating pain. Not at that moment. I don't remember feeling a goddamn thing. My legs just let go and I was on the floor. Hey, I'm a tough guy. In the ring, I was hit by bulldozers and I didn't go down. But there I was, suddenly on the floor like a crybaby, a pussy.

Maybe there was someone up there looking out for me. Maybe if I had stayed on my feet, Angel would have plunged the knife into my heart and finished the job. *Someone up there looking out for me?* Angel stepped over me and headed for the bathroom. I scrambled to my feet and stumbled to the night stand.

39

Angel tried the bathroom door. It was locked. I opened the drawer and retrieved the gun. Angel slammed his shoulder into the thin, wooden door and it shattered to pieces. I unloaded one, two, three thundering shots into his back. He stood tall for a brief moment like a statute being held up by the force of the shots and then collapsed to the floor. His head bounced off the tile floor of the john with his feet still in the bedroom. His body was draped over the base of the busted door.

Eva, cool and calm, not a whimper out of her, approached Angel and checked for a pulse. Hell, we both knew none would be there. She slapped a towel onto my gaping wound and instructed me to hold it tight, grabbed the vodka bottle, handed it to me and told me to chug. When I opened my mouth to question why, she hollered, "Drink!"

"Chug it! Drink it all!"

I gulped a mouthful.

"I've got to go to the hospital!" I exclaimed.

"No hospital! Drink!"

I drank like my life depended on it. Maybe it did!

Eva splashed some sort of liquid on a washcloth and pressed it against my wound. I let out an ungodly scream!

"Don't be a baby!" she chastised.

Tough broad!

Why the hell am I always so goddamn attracted to tough broads?

"Drink!"

And I did, I drank like crazy

My head swirled.

"I've got to go to the hospital!" I repeated.

"No hospital!"

I was somewhere between the moon and the other side of my mind when Eva stuffed a wet washcloth into my mouth and told me to bite. The next thing I knew she was sewing my wound and I goddamn nearly went through the ceiling.

"Bite!"

I might have passed out for a few moments, I don't know. But, suddenly, Eva wasn't sewing anymore and she was hustling, wiping things off and cleaning. She paid particular attention to Angel's knife, thoroughly washing and scrubbing the blade with soap and water and some other kind of liquid, then placing it back by his hand. But, then, almost like an afterthought, she took the blade back out of his hand, walked to her handbag and placed it inside.

I was groggy as all hell.

"We should call the cops!" I said.

"And tell them what? We just did them a big favor and executed *Mac the goddamn Knife!*"

"It was self-defense!"

"Yeah, three shots in the back. The cops are certainly going to agree that's self-defense!"

My head was so groggy, I had to think about that one; I had to think about what Eva was suggesting.

"Well, I was defending you!"

"Yeah, defending your lover against the guy she's been screwing for the past six months. Defending her in the victim's house, no less."

"This is Angel's house?"

"He pays the rent!"

My head was too groggy. I couldn't wrap my brain around that one.

The last thing she wiped clean was the gun. She put it on the floor; just as far from Angel as I was when I shot him.

Throughout it all, she was cool and calm, working the scene like a technician. She went to the phone, dialed a number, didn't say a word and hung up, just like she had when we arrived. My head was swirling. I had lost all concept of time, but I learned many months later that the call she attempted to make was at 10:20. But, hey, I'm getting way ahead of myself. We'll get to that later.

When she put the phone back in its cradle, we both got dressed. That's right, Eva was doing all this wiping and cleaning and adjusting

41

and she was still stark naked. I was drunk as a skunk; my head was reeling and I was in excruciating pain.

"Bring the bottle with you," she instructed. We were out of there in – what? – 15 minutes after the shooting. She wiped the door handle clean of prints as we left.

"Give me the keys," she instructed.

I couldn't find them. Turned out, I was reaching into the wrong pocket. Eva stuck her hand in the right one and pulled them out.

"I'll drive," I said.

"Yeah, you'll drive," she said sarcastically.

She opened the passenger door and guided me inside.

We pulled out and were rambling along that narrow, roughly paved road in the woods of Pawtucket, Rhode Island – the one we traversed on our way to the shack - when suddenly, there were headlights heading toward us. The high beams were on and the driver didn't bother to lower them. They were piercing and, in my drunken condition, they hurt like hell. Eva put a hand over her eyes. We passed the big black limousine that had those darkened windows and days later I had a vague memory of the passing car and figured that maybe I should have paid more attention at the time. But I didn't.

"I'm going to drive you to *The Palace*," Eva said.

"Why?"

"So you can walk to work in the morning. I'm going to have to take your car."

"Why are you taking my car?"

"I've got to get home somehow."

"Why don't you stay with me at *The Palace*?"

"Because there can't be any connection between us. We shouldn't be seen together. People shouldn't even know that we know each other. Not for a while. We can't hand the cops a motive for either of us for killing Angel."

"I'll have someone follow me back tomorrow and I'll leave it in *The Palace* parking lot for you. Or the lot at *The Examiner,* whichever you want."

I reached into my pocket and pulled out a crumpled pack of cigarettes. That, in itself; baffled me. I normally smoked Marlboros, which came in a box. The cigarettes I retrieved were Camels, which came in a soft pack and it was crumbled. I had no idea how I had come into possession of a crumpled pack of Camels. I just sort of shrugged my shoulders, though, and extracted a Camel. It took me several swipes of the match for it to light. When I finally accomplished it, I pulled a second butt from the pack, lit it off the first and handed it to Eva.

We were on the highway now. We drove for a few miles before either of us spoke again.

"Did you set that whole thing up with Angel at the house there in the woods?"

"Set what up?"

"The whole thing, Angel happening by when we were there together."

"Are you kidding? I could have been killed."

I took a long last drag on my cigarette, crushed it out and deposited it in the ash tray. Eva did the same.

"Yeah, that's true," I allowed. "But, still, you got what you wanted. You wanted me to kill Angel."

"Yeah, I got what I wanted. I wanted you to kill him before he killed me."

I took a final gulp from the vodka bottle, finishing it, and placed the empty on the floor in front of me.

"Drop me off at my apartment. I'm not so sure I'll be going to work in the morning anyway. I don't think I'll feel much like working."

"Go to work!" Eva insisted. "Don't do anything that might draw attention to you or make anyone think anything is wrong. Don't do anything different than you would normally do."

"I'd still rather you dropped me off at my apartment."

"And what would happen if your girlfriend happens to look out the window when I'm dropping you off?

"Don't worry about it. She's probably asleep."

We drove another couple of miles in silence. I shut my eyes. Damn, I was tired! Damn, I was hurting!

"I think I love you," she said.

I wasn't expecting that. That caught me totally off guard. I had no idea how to respond. So I didn't. My eyes were closed so I kept them closed and didn't say a thing. I was counting on her figuring I was sleeping. I even consciously tried to breathe heavily, the way I imagined I might sound if I was actually sleeping.

I think it worked. About five minutes later, she reached over, nudged me and said, "Wake up. We're in Brockton. I need directions to your apartment."

"You have to give me your telephone number," I said as we pulled up in front of my apartment building.

"I'm not going to do that," she said as the car rolled to a stop.

"Why not?"

"Because I don't want you calling me . . .

". . . It's not that I don't want you to call; it's just that – like I said – we've got to be very careful for a while right now. There can't be any connection between us. We can't let people know that we even know each other. I'll get in touch with you. Sometime when I'm at a safe phone, I'll call you at your work."

"Promise?"

"Of course."

Eva's head was cupped in my hand. I gently put pressure on the back of her head to guide it forward. I wanted to kiss her.

"No, I'm not going to kiss you. If she sees us kissing, it would only complicate matters."

I assumed Eva was referring to Barbara. I suppose she could see us from our second-floor apartment window, but it would be very unlikely that she'd be looking out at this very moment.

"OK, don't forget to call," I said.

"I promise . . . I won't forget," Eva assured me.

I opened the door slightly, turned to Eva, smiled and said, "Oh, by the way, I think I love you, too."

She leaped across the bench seat, grabbed me by the lapel, pulled me forward and, right then and there with my door still partially open and the interior light blazing, gave me the longest, most passionate, deeply abiding kiss of my life.

CHAPTER 7

MORE MOOD MUSIC

I staggered into the apartment and Guido was eating Cheetos and watching television. I had already learned my lesson about asking what he was doing up so late on a school night, so I didn't. I guess it was in the general neighborhood of 11:30 or quarter to 12, though. Maybe midnight.

Then Guido shocked the shit out of me. "Where you been?" he asked.

I couldn't believe it. Guido and I had always gotten along OK. Not great, like a loving father and son relationship, but there was never any kind of friction between us. Until that moment. There was something in his tone of voice I didn't like. Let alone the question.

"It's none of your business where I've been. I'm the adult; you're the kid!"

That came out of my mouth louder than I had intended.

"Have another drink!" Guido spat.

Probably louder than he had intended.

I walked into the bedroom. Barbara appeared to be sleeping. Good.

I went to bed, but didn't sleep. Still, I pretended to be sleeping when Barbara got up to use the bathroom. I didn't feel at all like talking. Not right then.

I guess Barbara didn't either. She took every precaution against making any noise that would wake me.

'Barbara fell back asleep very shortly after her head hit the pillow. It took me quite a while longer. The alarm woke us at 6 o'clock in the morning.

She didn't ask where I had been the previous night. I truly appreciated that.

I didn't take Eva's advice and report to work that day. I called in sick, saying I had a terrible pain in my gut, which of course, was the truth. What I didn't mention was that my head was pounding from the most severe hangover I had ever experienced.

Barbara gave me a rather passionate kiss before she left for work. Maybe that was her way of saying she forgave me for anything that may have happened the night before. Damn, if she only knew. . . She left the room simply telling me to "feel better." I figured I'd need a little help on that score so I searched the medicine cabinet and struck gold when I found some Percocet. *Take one every six hours as needed,* the directions read so I took two and mixed myself a drink. Strictly for medicinal purposes, I told myself, and besides, like the saying goes, it was 5 p.m. somewhere.

I placed a Leonard Cohen album on an old record player. Mood music. I can't remember any of the actual Leonard Cohen songs I was listening to the morning after the encounter with Angel. No, actually, that's not true. I remember one, *So Long, Marianne.* Leonard wrote it for Marianne Ihlen, a chick he had lived with for a time. They broke up and I think she married another guy. Leonard was saying goodbye in the song. I'm not certain whether he ever saw Marianne after the breakup. I sipped my vodka and thought about Eva. I wondered if I'd ever see her again. And, quite frankly, I doubted it. Hmmm, both Eva and I profess our love for one another, and now it's very possible that we'll never see each other again. That was really depressing. I thought about Leonard Cohen and I thought about Marianne Ihlen. Leonard Cohen once described Marianne as being intensely beautiful and I wondered if she could have been as intensely beautiful as Eva Green. And, quite frankly, I doubted that, too.

I staggered into *Ike's Café,* a gin joint down the street from the Superior Courthouse, late that afternoon. Hey, I couldn't go to *The Ambassador* where I was sure to run into *Examiner* people; not after calling in sick. The moment I walked in, I spotted Henry Nickalou sitting at a table with several other lawyers, a bottle of Miller Lite in front of him. I stood there and waited for Henry to notice me. When he did I nodded and then motioned to a vacant table a few feet away. Henry excused himself from the other attorneys and joined me at the table. A waitress happened by and I ordered another Miller Lite for Henry, a vodka and tonic for myself.

Henry, the hot shit, was smoking a corn cob pipe that particular afternoon. He generally looked like he'd be much more at home on a farm than in a courtroom, but this particular day the corn cob pipe and looking like he hadn't shaved in a few days, really put him over the top in that respect.

"You look like shit," Henry said.

"Thanks," I replied and I wanted to say something about look who's calling the kettle black, but I knew no matter how disheveled Henry might appear at the moment, I must have looked a hell of a lot worse. So I just left it at that.

I reached into the breast pocket of my shirt, produced a box of Marlboro's, took one out and lit it. God, it tasted good. My consumption of pills stood at five or six at the moment and, together with plenty of vodka, I was soaring higher than a kite and was feeling a hell of a lot better than I looked.

"What have you been doing, out celebrating the murder of your friend, Angelo Macrillo?" Henry asked.

The question hit me like a ton of bricks. I took a deep drag off my Marlboro. Said nothing. I must have looked at Henry inquisitively, because after a hesitation he added, "I heard about it on the radio."

Then Henry quickly added: "Wait a minute, didn't you know? Macrillo was murdered last night. They arrested some guy and charged him with the murder. They arrested him at the scene. Some guy named Maurice something or other."

All of that, obviously, made no sense to me whatsoever. Maurice arrested at the scene?

I had a vague memory of travelling along that dark, narrow road after the shooting and a big Lincoln passing us in the opposite direction. Eva blocking her face. I thought it was from the high beams invading her eyes, the same lights that were piercing my liquor-raked head.

Could that have been Maurice headed for the cottage?

Maybe.

"Maurice didn't kill Macrillo," I finally said.

And then after a proper hesitation for dramatic effect, I added, "I did."

"Shhh, keep your voice down, for God sake!" Henry scolded. "And don't say that to anyone ever again. Hell, if loose lips could sink ships you could have just sent the entire Kingdom of England's Royal Navy to Davey Jones's locker."

Then, this time keeping my voice down, I told Henry the entire story of the previous night in graphic detail.

"It sounds to me like this beautiful young maiden of yours was in such distress that she set the whole thing up," Henry philosophized.

I had to admit the thought had occurred to me. But, to Henry, I repeated what Eva had told me when I asked her about it.

"Naw, she could have been killed," I told Henry.

"But, she wasn't, was she?" Henry replied.

It wasn't until that night, the eve of Thanksgiving, 1975, sitting alone at home, drinking vodka and smoking cigarettes and weed, that I heard Maurice's last name for the first time. Guido was out with his friends and Barbara was. . . she was. . . I don't know where the hell she was or who she was with. But I was listening to a television news broadcast and I learned that, yes, of course, Henry had been correct and Maurice had been charged with the murder of Angelo "Angel" Macrillo.

"Maurice diMontiferro, who reportedly was arrested at the scene with the murder weapon in his hand, was arraigned in Providence Superior Court late this afternoon," the announcer said.

So that was Maurice's last name, diMontiferro. That was certainly a mouthful, even for a dude the size of *The Hulk*. If my name were Maurice diMontiferro, I think I'd change it.

CHAPTER 8
A MOST MEMORABLE THANKSGIVING

Barbara came home later that night, not as early as I would have preferred, but certainly sooner than I expected. Again, I didn't ask about where she had been or what she had been doing. We smoked a joint together.

The plan had been for me to spend the next day, Thanksgiving, with my mom and Barbara and Guido with Barbara's mother. We had never integrated family celebrations.

"Guido asked me if he could spend the holiday with a friend instead of going with me to his grandmother's," Barbara told me. "I said it would be OK."

"Ah-ha."

I had no clue why Barbara was telling me. Certainly, I had nothing to say about where Guido would be spending his holiday. But then she added: "I was wondering, I thought it might be a good idea if you and I spent the holiday together. I feel like we've been slipping apart lately and I thought it would be cool if we spend the day together, just the two of us."

I thought about it a few moments and agreed, "Yeah, I think that would be a great idea." I knew my mom, Frankie, would be disappointed, but it wasn't as if I was leaving her alone. Frankie was also spending the day with a couple of her siblings, my aunt and uncle. Same thing with Barbara's mom; she was spending the day with relatives, too.

"Yeah, I'd really like Thanksgiving, just you and me," I told Barbara and I sincerely meant it.

"Oh, good, I was hoping you'd say that. I scored a dime bag of coke we can do tomorrow," she said, cracking a very narrow smile out of the side of her mouth. Her brown eyes squinted. They squinted a lot. But on Barbara, it worked. Extremely sexy, really.

After we finished the joint, we made love, rolled over and went to sleep.

We slept late. Sometime long after the crack of dawn, Guido nudged the door open, cleared his throat and told us he was off to his friend's. After the rude awakening and hearing the front door slam so that we were well aware that Guido had, in fact, left the house, Barbara and I made love again and got up for breakfast, a line of coke apiece and a cup of steaming hot coffee, black. We spent most of the day in bed, snorting coke off a tiny makeup mirror, kissing and caressing and watching the *Macy's Thanksgiving Day Parade* on television. Barbara said it was very important for her to see the parade. Every year growing up, she watched it with her dad. It was a tradition. I had no particular interest in watching the parade and I'm not sure she did, either, other than the memory of watching it with her dad. But we cuddled in bed and watched the parade and felt very safe and secure and relaxed. We watched an old movie, *Love Story*, after the parade. Well, I say it was an *old movie*, but it was only about five years old at the time. It was a book before it was a movie, written by Erich Segal. I remember how Segal, who was supposed to be some kind of literary genius at Harvard, no less, took all kinds of criticism from the intellectual snobs he hung around with because he penned such a shallow and syrupy book. I had read it in about an hour and a half and I'm not a fast reader. Unlike Segal's high-polluting associates, though, I enjoyed it. The movie starred Ali McGraw and Ryan O'Neal. Barbara and I liked it.

After the movie, we crawled out of bed for Thanksgiving dinner. Barbara popped *Hungry Man* frozen dinners into the microwave: turkey, mashed potatoes and gravy for her and, because I never ate turkey, boneless ribs for me. You know, when I think of all the Thanksgivings of my life, I think the one I spent cuddling with Barbara, getting high, watching the *Macy's Thanksgiving Day Parade* and *Love Story* and eating frozen dinners, was my all-time favorite.

The next day I received a telephone call at work from my mother's brother, Father Richard Marchetta. That's right – can you believe it? – I've got an uncle who's a Roman Catholic priest. Anyhow Father Richard – or Uncle Richard, I was never really certain which one to call him so I frequently tried both of them on for size –called to say he was disappointed I hadn't spent Thanksgiving with my mom, him and their sister. And then he told me something that rocked my world. He said my mom told him last night that she was going to have to undergo some tests because the doctors found a spot on her lungs. I asked Father Richard how come Frankie hadn't told me, herself, and he said it was because she didn't want to worry me.

Yeah, that was just like Frankie alright.

He said Frankie asked him not to tell me, but he thought I had a right to know.

Then he went into this thing about how I should be paying more attention to my mom. I shouldn't be making her spend Thanksgiving without me. And I didn't think that was a fair criticism at all. Frankie and I were always extremely close and I spent plenty of time with her. Hardly a weekend ever went by without me spending time with her. So, one Thanksgiving came and went without me seeing her because I was repairing my relationship with the love of my life. That didn't seem fair that Father Richard should be giving me hell about that.

But Barbara and I celebrated the New Year a few weeks later in a very similar fashion as we did Thanksgiving. On New Year's Day, her father always insisted Barbara watch the Rose Bowl with him. So, Barbara and I got high, cuddled and watched UCLA and Ohio State in the Rose Bowl. I don't remember who won, but I suspect it may have been UCLA because I distinctly remember the camera capturing Ohio State head coach Woody Hayes on several occasions and every time he looked somewhat less than pleased.

I left the game a little early to run over and spend some time with my mom. Maybe that's why I don't have a clear recollection of who won. I never did see the end of it. But after Uncle Richard gave me a hard time about ignoring Frankie on Thanksgiving, I made it a point to spend some time with her on New Year's Day. Well, actually, it was New Year's night. It was nighttime before I got there. And Frankie wasn't feeling very well so I didn't stay long.

Those two holidays – Thanksgiving, 1975 and New Year's Day, '76 – marked a new beginning in the relationship between Barbara and me. It was as if we once again had discovered our own *Love Story*. I had never felt as close to anyone.

CHAPTER 9

ALWAYS THE GENTLEMAN

The next few weeks were golden. Charmed. The *new beginning* Barbara and I had discovered was heavenly. We spent every waking, non-working moment together enjoying the hell out of each other's company and every night we made wild, unbridled, passionate love.

Then I received a telephone call at work in February.

"Hello, Rocky."

It wasn't asked as a question, "Hello, Rocky?" It was a statement. She knew damn well who she was talking to.

And I didn't have to ask who was calling. I recognized her sultry voice instantly.

"Hello, Eva

"I was beginning to wonder if I was ever going to hear from you again," I said.

"I told you I'd call," Eva responded, not sounding at all challenged by my allegation. If anything, her voice was quite flirtatious. When I hesitated before adding another word, she said, "I told you that we'd have to be very careful; that we can't give the cops any reason at all to believe there's anything between us; not until Maurice is convicted of Angel's murder."

Again, I didn't say anything. I wasn't certain how I wanted to play this game. I wasn't even sure if I had been waiting and hoping to hear from Eva or not. Before I picked up the telephone, I thought

I had recently fallen in true love for the first time in my life with Barbara. But, come on, I was talking to the most exciting woman on God's green earth.

"I want you to know that I've been faithful to you; I haven't been with anyone," she said.

I sure as hell didn't know how to respond to that. When I didn't say anything, she continued, "I know you can't say the same thing. I know you're living with someone. I know you can't be faithful right now. Just tell me you still love me and still want me."

That was difficult at that particular moment. But I thought about those stunning blue eyes and that out-of-this-world figure and to my utter amazement, the words came out.

"Yeah, I love you, babe, and I'll always want you."

I felt her smiling over the line. I felt guilty and cheap as all hell.

Eva telephoned again in March and we renewed our vows.

But, getting back to more mundane matters, I wrote a column early in April, in which I questioned the integrity of some police officers in nearby Randolph who shot and killed a young black man who had been a suspect in an armed robbery. The cops claimed they were shooting in self-defense as they attempted to apprehend the suspect. But as it turned out the suspect was unarmed and, to make matters worse, they later learned he hadn't done the armed robbery in the first place. In the column, I questioned if the outcome would have been the same if the suspect had been white.

The day after my column appeared, another young black man with a cane hobbled into the newsroom, asking to speak to me. His name was Gregory Davies. The young man told me a story about how some Randolph cops had shot him in the leg and crippled him. It was an incredible story. *Incredible,* meaning *not credible,* not to be believed. Except I believed him. The reason I did was because he handed me a magazine that included an article detailing his saga. It described how Davies was driving his automobile in Randolph when he passed a police cruiser that was pulled to the side of the road. The cops had stopped a motorist. As Davies passed, his car backfired.

The cops believed Davies had taken a shot at them. They hustled back to the cruiser and pulled out. Davies stepped on the gas and sped away, the cruiser in hot pursuit.

Davies told me the reason he took off was because he had been drinking; he didn't want to get busted for operating under the influence of alcohol. He led the cops on a bit of a chase onto a highway and when he became convinced he wasn't going to outrun them, he pulled over. According to the cops, before that happened they saw Davies reach out the driver's side window and toss an object that they believed to be a handgun out and over his automobile. The weapon landed in a wooded area along the highway, they alleged. After pulling to a stop, Davies said he exited his vehicle, making certain his hands were up and in plain sight. The cops approached him with their guns drawn and a shot was fired into his kneecap.

Like I said, it was an incredible story; one that was very difficult to believe. But the magazine article that Davies handed me described how the cops did a search of the wooded area to the right of the highway and they did, in fact, find a gun. But the gun found behind a large rock, was so close to the rock that it was impossible to imagine how the gun could have landed there.

I might have taken the magazine article with a grain of salt. Hey, I wasn't born yesterday; I don't believe everything I read. But the publication was a prosecutors' magazine. You had to figure, if any slant was taken in a prosecutors' magazine, it would be in favor of the cops. I told Gregory he should sue the bastards.

He told me he didn't have money for a lawyer. I said he didn't need it. Any good attorney would take the case on a contingency basis. Of course, he would need a lawyer who was very good and would have the guts to take on the cops. I told him he should get Richie Egbert in Boston. The guy was damn good. I had seen him bring down a police chief in court.

I knew damn well that, as a newspaperman, it was my job to report the news. And as a columnist, it was my job to comment on it. It either case, it wasn't my job to make the news. But - what the hell? - sometimes when you see something so very wrong, you have to do something about it. I told Gregory Davies I'd make an appointment for him with Richie Egbert.

Gregory told me that would create a problem. As I might have suspected; he no longer had a driver's license.

I told him I'd drive.

You wouldn't believe our conversation on the way into Boston. Looking back on it, I don't believe it either. I told Gregory all about Barbara and how great she was and how lucky I felt to be with her and all that kind of shit. Syrupy as hell and you know me well enough to know I'm not a syrupy kind of guy. I sounded like a high school kid bragging about dating the captain of the cheerleading team. I don't know what got into me. Actually, that's not true. I do know what got into me. Pure unadulterated love. Despite the telephone calls from Eva, Barbara and I were still growing closer and closer and it seemed that I truly had found – if you'll excuse the expression – my *soul mate*.

Driving back from Boston, I told Gregory I'd probably be meeting Barbara at the *The Palace* lounge for a few drinks and asked if he wanted to join me and meet her. He said sure. The meeting was nothing that Barbara and I had talked about. If I wasn't home by a certain hour, she knew that I was probably at *The Palace*. If she wasn't home by a similar hour, she was probably there and we'd most likely end up meeting there.

The thing is, though, when Gregory and I arrived at the hotel, Barbara wasn't there. When she hadn't shown up after a couple of hours, I telephoned home. She wasn't there either. After a little while, the pay phone in the hallway outside the lounge rang and nobody else made a move toward it, so I left the bar to answer it. You got that right; it was Barbara.

"Hey, where are you, babe?" I asked.

"I'm out with an old friend," she replied. "He was looking to buy some pot. He called and asked if I could score some for him. So

I did. When we met so I could deliver it, he asked if he could buy me a drink."

A hundred questions should have poured through my head at that point. If this dude was such an *old friend,* where the hell did he get Barbara's telephone number? We hadn't been in our west side apartment all that long. We had a new telephone number. And where did this dude get the idea Barbara could score pot for him? What was she, a drug dealer back in the good ol' days when they knew one another? Yeah, all this shit should have been running through my head at that point, but I'm embarrassed to say it didn't. I guess I was just too much in love with Barbara and, after all, love is blind, isn't it? Hey she was my *soul mate.*

I told her to come to *The Palace.* Bring her *old friend* if she wanted.

"This is John Ripley," Barbara said.

He was tall, dark and (not very) handsome.

"It's a pleasure to meet you," I said with enough enthusiasm to give the impression it might, indeed, be a pleasure.

"Yeah, hi," he said, obviously not making the same effort.

"And this is my *new* friend, Gregory Davies," I said, nodding toward my companion.

"Yeah, hi," Barbara said.

Cold.

"Rocky's told me a lot about you, Barbara; all very, very good," Gregory said.

She didn't say anything in response. Maybe I detected the hint of a grunt.

We sat at the bar, Barbara to my left and her *old* friend to the left of her. Gregory was on my right.

Very little was said. Barbara had practically nothing to say and, when she did, she directed it toward John.

I was embarrassed as hell. She gave me a cold shoulder that was more frigid than the one that belonged to Frosty, the dude in the old top hat.

61

Obviously uneasy, Gregory excused himself and made his way to the pool table behind us. He racked the balls, selected a stick, chalked it and began to shoot.

I feel embarrassed telling you what happened next.

"Why don't you go play pool with your friend?" Barbara said.

There were probably dozens of appropriate responses I could have made – should have made – to put her in her place. But I didn't make any of them. I did the worst thing I possibly could have done. I got up and shot pool with Gregory. At the time, I rationalized it to myself. I told myself I actually felt like shooting pool right then.

By the time Gregory and I returned to the bar after our game, John Ripley had left. I can't honestly say that made me unhappy. Barbara was finishing her drink and said she was going home also. I told her that Gregory and I would finish our drinks, I'd give him a ride home and then I'd be right along.

She said, "Don't bother."

I told her, "Hey, it's no bother; I want to spend some time with you."

Gregory told Barbara it was nice meeting her.

Hell, I knew that was a lie.

Barbara muttered something in response. It was totally unintelligible.

There was little to say on the ride to Randolph when I drove Gregory home. I was embarrassed about Barbara's behavior after having bragged about how wonderful she was. I suppose I should have apologized for Barbara's conduct, but I didn't.

As soon as Gregory left the car and was out of sight, I whacked the steering wheel. Hard. I was goddamn angry. Seething. But I told myself that things would probably work out. Before our Thanksgiving celebration and our New Year's Day celebration, Barbara and I certainly had our share of disagreements. But we always worked them out. No matter what happened on any given day, no matter how angry we were at one another, we'd go to bed at night and make love. And it was as if our problems vanished.

Barbara loved sex. I loved sex. And we were both extremely good at it. We'd make love and all our problems would vanish. Gone.

Certainly that's what would happen this night.

I walked into our apartment. There was no Guido watching television and eating Cheetos. He was staying at a friend's.

I walked into our bedroom. Barbara was either asleep or pretending to be. But then I heard a gentle snoring that pretty much convinced me that she was, in fact, sleeping. I stripped off my clothes and cuddled up behind her. She reached back and attempted to push me away. Of course, I was too heavy for any of that kind of shit.

"Will you leave me alone?" she said, her voice dripping in utter exasperation.

"What's wrong with you tonight?" I asked in desperation.

"Nothing's wrong with me. You've been spending too much time with your sister."

"I don't have a sister!"

"You've been spending too much fucking time with your sister!"

It sounded like Barbara was talking ragtime. Maybe she was actually asleep when I arrived home. Maybe she was still half asleep now – without any idea of what she was saying. But this was the wrong night for that kind of bullshit. After the way she had embarrassed me at *The Palace*. She picked the wrong time to test my patience!

I leaped out of bed my fist clinched, feeling myself losing control. Barbara followed me right out of the bed and got into my face. We stood practically toe to toe, both of us naked as jay birds, while a full moon cast light into the otherwise darkened room.

"What the fuck are you talking about?" I screamed.

I don't remember her response, not the exact words. I just remember they didn't have anything to do with anything. She said something about my sister again and something about Gregory Davies. I wasn't really listening to what she said at this point so I couldn't quote her; I only remember the tone of her voice and I didn't like it at all. What was she so angry about? I didn't do a thing to her? She spat out a few more words and I whacked her across the face.

I'd like to tell you it was a slap, but it wasn't. It was more like a left hook only my hand was open; my fist wasn't clenched. But my elbow was locked and I whacked her pretty hard across the face. I was surprised she didn't go down. And even more surprised that she didn't shut up. She kept spewing shit. She said something about me being such a tough guy, hitting a girl. She knew I was a tough guy. She knew I had been a fighter and a good one. She saw me tangle with Irish Sean Casey, a heavyweight. But now she wouldn't shut up. Not even after I hit her. She just stood in front of me with her trap yapping.

I hit her again. Same thing, it was a vicious left hook, but with an open hand. I'm not proud. I'm embarrassed as hell telling you. Not proud at all; just telling you like it is. Like it was. And still she didn't shut up. Her face was crimson red now and she was crying frantically, but she didn't stop berating me, taunting me. She didn't show me any respect, absolutely no respect.

I hit her again. And maybe another time. I don't know. I wasn't keeping count. Still crying and still talking – screaming actually – she turned and walked away. I threw myself onto the bed. I wanted to cry myself out of anger and frustration and despair, but I wouldn't; I couldn't give her the satisfaction of seeing me cry. She threw on some clothes.

You bastard!" she muttered through clenched teeth. And she left the apartment.

After the door slammed behind her, I put on some clothes and laid on the bed, taking some deep breaths – chain smoking - and waiting for the police. Surely she'd go to the cops and they'd come to arrest me.

After an appropriate amount of time had passed, I felt confident Barbara wasn't returning with the cops, I got up, stripped and got back on the bed sweating profusely. I tried to make sense out of what had just happened. I tried to make sense out of what had taken place the whole night. I couldn't.

The apartment door swung open. Two seconds later, Barbara and some other chick she worked with walked into the bedroom. There I was, in all my naked glory, lying on my back with an ashtray on my chest and a butt hanging out of the corner of my mouth. I guess I should have been embarrassed, getting caught like that. I should have jumped off the bed and threw on a pair of jeans or grabbed a robe, but I didn't. I took my time getting up.

Barbara began gathering some of her things.

"I'm leaving you," she spat.

"I'll leave the key on the kitchen table."

"Don't," I said. "I'll go."

Of course I wouldn't let Barbara be the one to leave. That was me, always the gentleman.

CHAPTER 10
PHIL AIN'T MARCHING ANYMORE

I suppose the natural thing to do would have been to throw on some pants. But I didn't. I took my time retrieving a suitcase and then another one. Naked as a jaybird.

"You can go now, Gloria," Barbara said to her friend. "Thanks."

"I'll wait for *him* to leave," Gloria responded, not attempting to hide the disgust in her voice.

"It's OK, he won't hit me again, I'm sure," Barbara said.

"I'll wait," Gloria insisted.

After the two suitcases were filled, I took my time putting on jeans and a shirt and took the luggage out to my car. Then I returned to retrieve some suits on hangers, ties and a bunch of toiletries; all of which were tossed into my trunk. And, oh yeah, a tiny, yellow record player and some long-playing albums. All of my life's possessions in three short trips to the Karmann Ghia! Before leaving, I tossed my apartment key on the kitchen table and told Barbara to "have a nice life."

Barbara didn't respond.

Gloria did.

"You know, you're a real asshole!"

I guess I deserved that.

"Thanks for being here for Barbara," I responded to her.

I didn't know where I was going to go. I drove to the *Palace Hotel*, parked in the lot, and stretched out across the backseat of my car. It took quite a while to get to sleep.

The thunder startled me! I looked out the window at the belt buckle of the tallest, biggest cop in the world. The Billy club he had used to rap on my car roof and cause the thunder was firmly grasped in his hand. As soon as my weary eyes reached the cop's face, I knew him right away, Johnny Pellegrino.

Johnny Pellegrino's parents and my parents were good friends a very long time ago, probably before I was a glimmer in my old man's eye. Johnny's father was a bus driver, which was what my father did after his fighting career. They worked for the same bus company. Our parents hung out a lot together. And after my father died and Johnny's mom died; Johnny's father and Frankie hooked up for a while. I have no idea how that relationship ended. I think maybe Johnny's father died or something.

Johnny Pellegrino, towering above me with a Billy club clutched in his hand, looked down and exclaimed, "Oh, Rocky, it's you!"

I suppose I should have been embarrassed – getting caught sleeping there in my car like a homeless dude – but I wasn't. Hey, for all intents and purposes, I was homeless. At that particular moment I was homeless, anyway.

Johnny mumbled something, turned on his heels and walked away. I went back to sleep.

It was the rising sun that woke me. I had no idea what time it was. I took some stuff from the backseat of my car, entered the *Palace Hotel* from the back door and shaved and washed up as best as I could in the men's room sink. I put on a dress shirt and tie, a pin-striped suit, took my time eating breakfast at some greasy spoon and attended my mother's funeral. Yeah, Frankie had passed away a couple of days prior. It happened pretty fast after she was first diagnosed.

Father Richard Marchetta presided at his sister's – my mother's - funeral. After the service, he invited everyone to the home of his other sister, Philomena Marchetta-Russo. I didn't go. I'm certain Uncle Richard was extremely disappointed and totally bullshit that I didn't show up at his sister's that day, but I had to find a place to live. I'm certain that Frankie, if she were alive, would totally understand why I didn't go to the gathering at Aunt Philomena's.

I knew John Livingston, my friend at work, had left his wife recently and a Realtor had helped him find a place where the price was right. But, to be perfectly honest, I didn't know if a place existed where the price would be right for me. I had no first month's rent, no last month's rent and no security deposit. I had been a kept man since I left my wife. I didn't contribute toward the rent or any of the household expenses. I turned most of my paycheck over to Susan for child support. About the only thing I took care of was our bar bill, Barbara's and mine. We ran a tab at *The Palace.* Many weeks, I found that tab difficult to handle.

John Livingston gave me the name and telephone number of the Realtor who had helped him, Charles Buttonwood. "You can call me Button or you can call me Woody, just don't call me Late for Breakfast," he mused when I telephoned him. "Or Chuck, don't call me Chuck; I don't like Chuck." The dude was a complete asshole.

"OK, Chuck," I responded. "I'm looking for a place to stay . . . as of yesterday."

I outlined my finances – or lack of them – and asked Chuck if he could help me.

"You don't want to live on Green Street," he said more as a statement of fact than a question.

But when he waited for a response, I gave him one.

"Hey, beggars can't be choosers," I replied. "I'll live anywhere."

Green Street was a hop, skip and a very small jump from *The Examiner,* almost directly across Main Street from it. I had never paid much attention to the old, broken down rooming houses before and most certainly had never pictured myself living in one of them, but what the hell?

"Do you have something on Green Street?" I asked.

69

"No, not me," the dude responded. "But go see Big George. Big George is the building manager for several of the houses on Green Street. He'll probably have something available."

"How do I get hold of this Big George" I asked. "Do you have his phone number?"

"I don't even know if he has a phone. Just go to Green Street and ask anybody you see there for Big George. Everybody on Green Street knows him. And there are always people out and about."

So I headed out of the newspaper and crossed Main Street. I immediately spotted none other than Bobby the Car Thief making his way down Green Street. Bobby was a friend of a friend who I occasionally drank with at one watering hole or another. I don't think I ever knew his last name, but his propensity to drive away with automobiles that didn't belong to him was somewhat legendary to one and all so everybody always referred to him simply as Bobby the Car Thief.

"Hey, Rocky my man, how are you doing?" Bobby spat as he approached. He was about my height, skinny, clean-shaven and combed his brown hair straight back over his head. He needed a haircut badly. He was wearing a t-shirt, dungarees and an old Army fatigue jacket. I kind of doubted if Bobby had ever served in the Army. He didn't seem the type.

"I've had better days," I admitted. "Hey, do you know a guy around here, Big George?"

"Of course, everyone knows Big George. What do you want him for, drugs or a place to stay?"

"A place to stay."

"You wanna move onto Green Street?"

But, before he gave me a chance to respond, he told me to be careful; don't stay too long.

"It's a wonderful place to live," Bobby allowed, "but the lifestyle can be addictive and, in the long run, it will kill you. If you're alone and nothing to do on a weekend night, just take a stroll along Green Street. Someone is bound to invite you in for a drink or to smoke a little weed or, if you're really lucky, to partake in some shit-kicking drugs. And the broads on Green Street are friendly and horny as hell. At one time or another, every guy on Green Street goes to bed with every broad on Green Street.

"But," he warned again, "don't stay too long, it will kill you."

He didn't specify what would kill me. Drugs or AIDS, I surmised.

"So where do I find Big George?" I asked.

Bobby glanced over my shoulder and told me to turn around. Three dudes were walking down the street. Two of them were of pretty average height and weight and the other was the size of a garage.

"I guess I don't have to ask you which one is Big George, do I?"

"No, you don't."

When I approached George, I introduced myself and told him what I wanted. He said he'd meet me in an hour at 113 Green Street. The other end of the block, on the corner of Warren Ave. He'd show me the room.

"Whoa, wait a minute; what's it going to cost me?" I asked.

"Thirty-five dollars a week."

That fit into my budget . . . like a glove.

Big George didn't even seem embarrassed – not fazed in the slightest - when he showed me the room and a cockroach meandered across the floor. I certainly had the distinct impression that, if I had said anything about it, he would have asked me what the hell I expected. The place was one fairly large room that served both as a bedroom and living room and there was a tiny kitchenette off to the side. Bedroom? Hell, that consisted of a rather thin and somewhat dirty mattress on the floor, immediately to your left as you walked inside. A common bathroom for the use of everybody on the second floor of the three-floor, run-down, wood-framed apartment building, was out the door and down the hall.

It didn't matter that there wasn't a private bath or the joint was cockroach infested or any of that shit. I would have taken it sight unseen. The price was right.

This was a Friday so at least I'd have a couple days over the weekend to move into my new room and get situated. Hmmm. A couple of days to get situated? All it took was a few minutes that Friday night. Unload my clothing and shit from the trunk of my Karmann Ghia and lug it up to the second floor of 113 Green Street. Then run over to the "packie" on the next block– "packie," that's Boston talk for a liquor store – grab a bottle of vodka and some tonic and tote it back to my room. I mixed a drink, put a long playing record on the tiny player and listened to Phil Ochs tell the world he ain't marching anymore.

Phil Ochs was one of those folk singers that came along in the sixties and seventies who spoke out against the war in Vietnam, bigotry and everything that was evil in the world. He was a hero of mine. I could listen to him for hours. Which I did that night. I listened to Phil Ochs and a little bit of Dylan and Jaime Brockett, but mostly to Phil. I drank vodka and chain-smoked Marlboros. Every now and then, I'd get up and shadow box a little bit. Right there in my second-floor room. Feeling down. My mother's funeral earlier that day. Barbara, the love of my life gone.

Forever.

I attempted to drink and shadow box my troubles away.

Saturday. What the hell was I going to do? Sit in my room alone, smoke cigarettes, finish off the bottle of vodka that was practically empty, shadow box and listen to Phil Ochs some more? No, that would be too depressing. Had to get out. Drink in a drinking establishment. But I really didn't feel like conversing and mingling so much. So I left the flophouse and traipsed along Green Street, across Main Street and down to *The Ambassador*. It was Saturday. People got out of work early. They didn't stop in to drink on Saturday. They wanted to get home and begin the weekend with their families.

I sat at the bar. Alone. The television high on a wall at the end of the bar. I could hear it. A few people in and out. Nobody I knew. Not well enough to say hi to anyway. The TV was turned to the news. It was there, smoking cigarettes and steeped in my depression, drowning my sorrows that I heard the news anchor describe how the body of Phil Ochs was discovered hanging in his sister's Far Rockaway, Queens, home the day before. He had committed suicide at age 35.

I had always told myself that suicide was a coward's way out. I suppose that was kind of easy to say when things weren't going haywire. When your mother hadn't died. When the woman you loved with all your heart had cheated on you. And then you whacked her around, something you previously couldn't imagine ever doing. And then the same woman – the same one you loved with all your heart – throws you out. Yeah, it's easy to say killing yourself is the easy way out before you're feeling totally down and totally out and then Phil Ochs, your hero, takes his own life and it gets you thinking about it. Yeah, I thought about it. But, come on now, what Phil Ochs did wasn't no easy way out. Hanging yourself? Shit, that's scary as hell. If I were ever going to kill myself, I wouldn't do it by hanging. Damn, can you imagine what kind of trauma would be going through your mind when you're hanging there, choking and you can't do a damn thing about it. Hanging yourself is crazy.

So I sat there at the Ambassador, smoking cigarettes and drinking vodka and tonics, wondering what time Phil had taken his life. Had he died at the very moment I was sitting in my room listening to him on a long-playing album that was scratched in places. Oh, yeah, I guess I didn't mention that before, did I? The record was scratched in a couple of places and there was an occasional thump! thump! thump! accompanying some of his songs. Now that's depressing! You oughta be able to listen to Phil Ochs without a thump, thump, thump! Anyhow, I wondered if old Phil killed himself at that very moment. The news story I heard didn't specify the time of day it happened.

CHAPTER 11

THE BIG-BONED, OLD OKIE GIRL

When I walked back to my new home at 113 Green Street, I let myself into the building with the key I had been provided, but before going up to the second floor, I stopped and knocked on the door of Big George's first-floor apartment. I wanted to report a leak in the pipe under my kitchen sink. To call it a leak, though, would be a gross understatement. When you turned on the water in the kitchen, it gushed onto the floor. To tell you the God's honest truth, it really didn't bother me all that much, but I figured left unattended, it wouldn't be long before the water found its way through the floor and into the room below.

A big-boned, large-chested, old Okie girl responded to my knock. Well, she wasn't all that old. A few years my senior. And I don't know that she was from Oklahoma. She talked with some sort of a down-country accent. Hell, she could have been from Alabama, for all I know. She had hazel eyes and a warm smile.

"Is Big George in?" I asked.

She responded, "No," and then there was an awkward pause.

"Is there something I can help you with?" she finally asked. "I'm George's girlfriend."

"My name's Rocky Scarpati. I'm a new tenant on the second floor." Then I went on to tell her how the pipe under the kitchen sink gushed and I told her it didn't bother me all that much, but I was afraid it might flood the room underneath.

Sarah, that was her name I later learned, told me she appreciated my reporting it. "I'm sure if George was here, he'd tell you he'll take care of it. So I know that's what he would want me to say. He'll take care of it and thanks for letting us know."

Yeah, a very warm smile.

Two days later on Monday, I was leaving *The Examiner* by the front door, which was kind of a new thing for me. I had always left by a rear-side door because my car would be parked in the lot across Ward Street. Either that or I'd be stopping for a drink at *The Ambassador* out behind the newspaper. But now my room was on Green Street, which was almost directly across Main Street. When I left the paper this Monday afternoon by the front door, Barbara was waiting for me in her big blue *boat* parked illegally in front of *The Examiner.* She drove an old, beat-up Chrysler or Oldsmobile. It was a big, blue thing. I wondered how Barbara knew to wait *in the front* of the newspaper. If it was actually me she was waiting for. She certainly didn't know I had scored a room on Green Street. So, how did she know enough to wait in front of the newspaper? But I didn't ask.

I opened the passenger door and sat inside.

"What are you doing here?"

"I don't know; I guess I wanted to see you."

She was wearing huge dark glasses.

"If someone had just done to me what I did to you, I wouldn't want to see him."

There was a pregnant, awkward silence.

Finally, I said, "Take off the glasses."

Her eyes were swollen, practically closed, discolored beyond belief.

"Did I do that?" I exclaimed.

"Who the hell do you think did it?"

"I didn't mean it that way. I just meant – I don't know – I just meant that I didn't realize I hit you *that* hard."

"Well, you did!"

I was careful not to say sorry. I'll admit, I felt guilty as hell and like an asshole, but I wasn't sorry. Not really. She had put me down really bad in front of my new friend. Made me feel like a total jerk. I wished I hadn't hit her. But I was kind of glad that I did. If ever anyone did, she had it coming.

"So why are you here?"

"I thought maybe you'd buy me a drink."

I couldn't believe what I was hearing.

"That's not a good idea," I told her.

"Probably not. But you wouldn't hit me in a barroom. I thought maybe you'd want to buy me a drink. Maybe we could talk a little bit."

"That's not a good idea," I repeated.

I didn't want to get close to Barbara. I didn't want it to happen again.

"You're probably right," Barbara conceded.

"I'll see you around," I said.

And left the car.

I ran into Big George as I was walking up Green Street. A television set, radio, a lot of clothing and several pairs of underwear and old shoes were on the brown grass in front of the rooming house. I asked George what that was all about and he told me he had evicted Rick, the tenant in 1C. A hundred questions swarmed into my mind, but I didn't ask any of them. I came to learn that was just the usual way George had of evicting tenants. He merely left their stuff in front of the building.

"Did Sarah tell you about the pipe under my kitchen faucet?" I asked. Again, I told him it didn't bother me all that much, but I was afraid it might cause greater damage.

"Yeah, she told me," George allowed. "I'll take care of it."

The remainder of that week was unseasonably warm. I opened my windows at night, turned on a fan and welcomed the warm breeze. I could hear the jukebox from *The Mission*, a barroom a block away on Legion Parkway. There was a small wooded area – perhaps downtown Brockton's one and only wooded area – between Green Street and *The Mission,* but still the country music on the juke box was coming through loud and clear.

Jump ahead now to Saturday night and it was probably the music from the same jukebox that lured me to *The Mission*. I never really consciously decided to go there. I just left my room and started meandering and that's where I ended up. The place was pretty crowded when I walked in and Frankie Valli was telling some chick on the jukebox how much his eyes adored her. Bobby the Car Thief was at a corner table playing liars' poker with a couple of degenerates and then I noticed Sarah sitting at the bar, apparently alone. I drifted her way and she told me to sit down, buy her a drink.

I did both of those things.

I mentioned the leak under the kitchen sink again and Sarah told me it would never get fixed.

"I thought you said Big George would fix it," I noted.

"No, I told you he would want me to tell you he'd fix it and that's what he would say to you. He always says he's gonna fix things. But he never does. Nothing on Green Street ever gets fixed."

I asked her where Big George was and she told me he was probably out with some bimbo getting laid if he was lucky.

When we finished our drinks, Sarah bought me one. And that's how we spent the time until about midnight; I'd buy her a drink; she'd buy me one back.

About the time Glen Campbell was talking about knowing every crack in the dirty streets of Broadway, Sarah said she was going to call it a night. I said I'd walk her home and that's how we came to leave just as Glen was feeling "Like a Rhinestone Cowboy, riding out on a horse in a star-spangled rodeo."

When we headed out the front door, I started down Legion Parkway toward Warren Avenue to follow it over to Green Street. Sarah said she'd show me a shortcut and led me beside *The Mission* to the narrow wooded area behind it. We followed a small dirt pathway. Just as we were about to emerge from the trees, there was a fat, old log right across the pathway. Sarah stepped over it and then sat down on it.

I sat beside her.

She turned to me and kissed me passionately. Almost violently. Certainly, something beyond seductive.

When our mouths parted, she exclaimed: "I want you."

I told her I'd like that, too.

She said go along to my room. She'd follow me in about five minutes.

I guess it was about 2 or 3 o'clock in the morning that she left my room and went to hers.

Eight, maybe nine o'clock the next morning, there was a gentle knock on my door.

I threw on my robe.

It was Sarah who whisked inside. As much as a big-boned, old Okie girl could "whisk," anyway.

"Take off your robe and lay back on the mattress," she instructed. "I'm going to service you."

She quickly disposed of her clothing.

When I reached for her breast, she objected.

"No, I don't want you to do anything. I told you, I'm gonna take care of you."

"Shit, I must have been really good last night," I said.

She flashed that warm smile of hers, winked and nodded affirmatively.

CHAPTER 12

THE GENIUS OF TOM WAITS

Well I hope I don't fall in love with you
'Cause falling in love just makes me blue
Well the music plays and you display your heart for me to see
I had a beer and now I hear you calling out for me
And I hope that I don't fall in love with you.

That's the first verse of the most beautiful song ever written. It was by Tom Waits, who did a little bit of rock and a little bit of blues and, I guess, some experimental jazz, but I always thought of him and loved him as a folk singer. He delivered emotion-shattering, down-under magical lyrics in a gravelly, gritty voice. My favorite Tom Waits' song was the one I quoted above. I thought about it, about the time I left the lounge at *Capeway*, which was a restaurant on Main Street in Brockton. It was the early morning hours of Sunday, a week after my most illicit rendezvous with Big George's live-in girlfriend.

In the previous week, I had received two telephone calls at work from Barbara. Both calls came in when I was attempting to meet deadline, so I had to cut them drastically short. I didn't want to talk to her because I missed the hell out of her and she insisted she missed me. I figured if we talked too much, we'd end up getting back together and, at some point in time, I'd wind up beating the shit out of her again. Obviously, I wouldn't intend to, but if I got to drinking and Barbara got to cheating, both of which were pretty certain to happen, I'd end up losing it again and smacking her.

During the same week, I also received a telephone call from Eva and that one, too, was when I was on deadline, but I didn't cut that conversation short. It had been a long time since her last call and I was longing to hear her voice and a confirmation that she was still thinking about me. I told her that Barbara and I had broken up and she sounded genuinely happy about that and said that she now expected I would remain faithful and true to her. Just as she was to me, she repeated. I had no way of knowing, of course, if that were true and, quite frankly, found it hard to imagine that it could be, but I said sure, I was all hers now and I'd remain forever faithful. When I finally got off the line from Eva, I was beyond deadline and the page I was editing was late, but they couldn't put out the newspaper without a page two so, obviously, it delayed the printing.

The managing editor, Hugh Beckerman, a crusty, old, whiskey-guzzling bastard, wasn't very happy about the late arrival of page two, but there wasn't all that much he could do about it. He grimaced and snarled, "Goddamnit, Scarpati, don't let it happen again!" but what the hell was he going to do, fire me?

So, I was at *Capeway* when I was reminded of that beautiful Tom Waits' song. *Capeway* was known for its prime rib; it had a fantastic prime rib and its lounge was open late into the night and early into the next morning. It was something between a singles' bar and a night club. The house band consisted of several dudes who played instruments and a pretty, somewhat sexy and semi-talented girl vocalist.

I don't know exactly what brought me to *Capeway* that particular Saturday night. I suppose you could call it fate, but that wouldn't necessarily be true. I dropped in from time to time for a drink or five and to dance the night fantastic.

I sat at the bar, sipping my drink and chain smoking, when I noticed this chick – this very attractive chick - sitting at a table close by. She had dark hair – a pixie-cut with striking bangs – I guess my days of lusting only after women with blonde hair – long blonde hair at that – were, indeed over. This chick's dark hair shined; shit, it practically sparkled. Actually, had kind of a blue tinge to it. Her large, dark eyes were heavily made up – perhaps too heavily made up – and her full, pouty lips were very red. Perhaps too red. But she still was a knockout. She certainly captured my attention. Voluptuous! And she had a body that wouldn't quit. As my good friend, Tony Lombardi, used to say, "She was built like a brick shithouse and not a brick outta place."

Again from the first verse: *Well the music plays and you display your heart for me so see.*

I had a beer and now I hear you calling out for me . . .

Yeah, the music was playing and I saw the goddess looking at me; devouring me. It reminded me of that night with Eva months ago at *The Ambassador,* a night I wished never happened.

But I was convinced that this chick. for all intents and purposes, was *displaying* her *heart for me to see."*

No, I didn't have a beer as the song suggests. I had given up beer a very long time ago. I was drinking vodka now. But, yeah, I swear that I heard her *calling out for me.* She was telling me to get my ass over to her table and introduce myself. I didn't have my co-workers sitting with me, aggressively nudging me to go over and meet her the way I did the night I approached Eva Green at *The Ambassador.* So, this particular night at *Capeway,* I didn't meander over and introduce myself to this mysterious beauty. Not quite yet, anyway.

Well, the room is crowded, people everywhere
And I wonder should I offer you a chair?
Well if you sit down with this old clown
I'll take that frown and break it
Before the evening's gone away I think that we could make it.
And I hope that I don't fall in love with you.

Yeah, the room was certainly crowded. I couldn't very well offer the lady a chair, though. Hell, she was the one sitting at a table. I was at the bar. But, of course, the intellectual-looking dude with the white bushy hair and moustache sitting with her might have something to say about that. He was smoking, smoking a pipe.

But, still, as the Waits' melody suggests, I nonetheless had the strong impression that if she sat down with this old clown, I'd take that frown and break it. Hell, I don't even know if she was wearing a frown. I don't remember a frown. But I was very convinced that *before the evening's gone away we could make it.* I had that fantasy about a lot of girls I met for the first time back then. Still, this chick was something special.

Unlikely as it might sound under the circumstances, I hoped I wouldn't fall in love with her. I had enough entanglements with Barbara and Eva. I didn't need another woman in my life. And I was always so totally impulsive and quick to fall in love. I didn't need that shit on this particular night.

Well the night does funny things inside a man
These old Tom-cat feelings you don't understand
Well I turn around to look at you
You light a cigarette
I wish I had the guts to bum one
But we never met
And I hope that I don't fall in love with you.

Yeah, I turned and she was lighting a cigarette. Obviously I had no urge to bum one. I was chain smoking rather furiously myself, one Marlboro after the next. Drinking vodka. Listening to the music. Getting into the mood. Getting into the mood for exactly what, I wasn't very sure.

I can see that you are lonesome just like me
And it being late, you'd like some company

84

Well I turn around to look at you and you look back at me
The guy you're with he's up and split
The chair next to you is free
And I hope that you don't fall in love with me.

Hell, obviously I had no way of knowing if this chick was lonesome like me. At one point when I looked over at her, Albert Einstein, who had been sitting with her, had up and left.

Yeah, the chair next to her at this point was free. But I didn't go and sit in it. Sometimes there's just no excuse for my actions! Or inactions!

Now it's closing time, the music's fading out
Last call for drinks; I'll have another stout.

You know, I can't ever remember drinking in a joint, any joint at any point in my life, when they had *Last Call* and I didn't order another drink.

Well I turn around to look at you
You're nowhere to be found
I search the place for your lost face
Guess I'll have another round
(But, then again, how could I? They already had Last Call.)
And I think that I just fell in love with you.

We all knew that that was going to happen, didn't we? We all knew, at some point, I was going to look for this beautiful, overly made-up chick and she was going to be gone. And I'd be regretting it. And that's exactly what happened sometime after Last Call that night. And I regretted it. I think it was exactly at that point that I thought about the Tom Waits song – the most beautiful song ever written. Tom Waits is a genius.

CHAPTER 13
I'LL BE WATCHING YOU

I stumbled up the stairs to my second-floor room. I'm not certain what time it was. It all runs together during the early morning hours when you've been drinking heavily. I unlocked the door to my room and staggered inside to find Sarah, lying there naked, asleep on the mattress on my floor. Sarah, the big-boned ol' Okie girl, Big George's girlfriend, covered with a sheet and blanket. She was asleep, her shirt, dungarees, bra and panties on the floor next to her. It was a pretty chilly April night. I stripped off my clothes, put them next to Sarah's on the floor and lay down beside her.

My arrival awakened her.

"Where have you been?" she asked, rubbing her eyes.

"Out; I didn't realize we had a date."

"We didn't. George and I had a fight. He took off. I'm sure he's with one of his bimbos. I came here. I hope you don't mind."

I wasn't sure if it would have made a hell of a lot of difference if I did mind.

We then made crazy, unbridled sex. It was pretty exciting. I imagined I was with the chick I had just almost met at *Capeway*.

Sometime after daybreak, I was awakened by a tiny stone against my second-floor window. I looked out the window to see Barbara about to toss another one. I motioned to her that I'd be right down. I rushed to put on my dungarees, jersey and loafers. I should have

87

grabbed a jacket, too. The unseasonably warm streak had snapped and it was rather chilly.

"What's this all about?" I asked.

"I've been missing you," she responded.

"How did you know which room was mine?"

"You pointed it out to me before."

I didn't recall that.

But I didn't question her any further about it, either.

We were both silent for a moment . . . a long moment. I shivered a bit from the chill. What was she expecting . . . me to invite her up to my room?

"You hungry? You want to get some breakfast?" I asked.

She nodded.

We walked along Green Street, took a right onto Main and entered a tiny greasy-spoon diner named, appropriately enough, *The Greasy Spoon*. It was the same place I had had breakfast the morning of my mother's funeral. As appropriate as its name seemed, I always questioned the wisdom of calling it that.

I ordered sausage, home fries and eggs over easy. It was the first time I had ordered my eggs over easy since I was a kid. I didn't like them when I was a kid and I didn't like them this particular day either. I wasn't so fond of sausage, either. Particularly *The Greasy Spoon's* sausage; it had a bitter taste. I think I subconsciously ordered breakfast that way because I didn't want to enjoy it very much with Barbara. I was afraid of feeling too good in Barbara's company because I didn't want to get back together. Everybody knows that's a bad idea. Anybody who has ever watched any crime shows on TV knows that as soon as a guy hits a chick and they get back together, the dude always does it again. Just like Angel did with the beautiful Eva Green. And when it happens again, it escalates. The chick gets beaten worse. And she keeps coming back and he keeps beating her worse until maybe he kills her. That's just the way it always happens. And I didn't want any part of spending the next 25 years or so in prison.

I swear, if they ever make a movie about this book, they'd be playing *Every Breath You Take* by The Police in the background. It's about a star-crossed obsessed lover who is stalking the object of his-her affection:

Every breath you take
Every move you make
Every bond you break
Every step you take
I'll be watching you.

Every single day
Every word you say
Every game you play
Every night you stay
I'll be watching you

Oh can't you see
You belong to me
My poor heart aches
With every step you take.

I'd like to tell you that The Police tune was playing on the jukebox while I was sitting there at *The Greasy Spoon* not enjoying breakfast. But, of course, that would be quite impossible. This was the spring of 1976 and it would be another seven years before *Every Breath You Take* would be released.

"How was *Capeway* last night?" Barbara asked.

"What the hell, have you been following me?" I asked with all the amazement and indignation I could muster at the moment.

"Not at all," she responded. "I just happened to be driving by and I saw you walking in. And then, later in the night, I saw your car still parked in the parking lot."

The parking lot was behind *Capeway;* behind the restaurant. You couldn't see it *just driving by.* You'd have to be looking for it.

"You just happened to be driving in the parking lot. In the parking lot *behind* the restaurant," I said.

Barbara ignored the comment.

We parted company after breakfast. Barbara looked like she was expecting a kiss goodbye before we parted. I'm not exactly sure how a person looks when she's expecting a kiss and I'm not exactly sure how to describe it to you now but she did and I didn't give her one, I didn't kiss her goodbye.

CHAPTER 14
HE'S NO PAUL NEWMAN

The following weekend - Saturday - I spent most of the afternoon in my room, smoking cigarettes and drinking vodka and getting depressed as hell listening to Phil Ochs and Jamie Brockett and Tom Waits – particularly Tom Waits singing *I Hope I Don't Fall in Love With You*. I was thinking a lot about the heavily-made-up doll who couldn't appear to take her eyes off of me and the opportunity I missed the Saturday prior. And I said to myself, "Shit, I gotta get out!" I thought of going to *Capeway* again, hoping the raven beauty from the previous week would be there again, but figured she wouldn't and that would simply make me uncontrollably depressed. So I drifted on over to *The Mission*.

I don't know what I had in mind, I really don't. I don't know if I was hoping to run into Sarah or the music on the juke box was just so alluring.

As I walked into the joint, Sammy Davis Jr. was explaining to the world *who can take a sunrise, sprinkle it with dew; cover it with choc'late and a miracle or two*. I immediately scanned the bar, looking for Sarah. And I immediately spotted her. Sitting there right next to Big George. And I thought to myself that this could be extremely awkward, but when I asked myself why it should be and I couldn't come up with a reasonable response; I joined them at the bar.

I sat down, ordered them each another beer – they both had been drinking Schlitz - and myself a vodka and tonic. Sarah flashed me that million dollar smile of hers. That was one thing about Sarah. She may not have been slim. She may not have been beautiful. Not even particularly charming. But she had an extremely pleasing smile.

George poured the beer into the glass that was sitting on the bar in front of him. He took a large swig, scowled and let loose a huge burp. Sarah drank from the bottle. She gulped a good amount and placed the bottle, rather hard, back onto the bar. She swiped her mouth with the back of her hand. At least she didn't belch.

I lit a Marlboro and asked Big George how he was doing and George told me he was doing just fine and Sarah quickly chimed in that that was a lie and challenged her boyfriend to tell me the truth.

"No, really, I'm doing fine," Big George insisted, sounding perturbed that Sarah had corrected him, but she forged on, saying, "Tell him, George. Tell him what's bothering you. You know you're not just fine."

George gritted his teeth, shook his head and said, "I got arrested a little ways back. I'm scheduled to go to trial Tuesday. I think I'm gonna be spending some time behind bars."

"Tell me about it, George. What did you do?"

"There's nothin' to tell really," George said. "I just did something really stupid. There's nothin' to tell."

"Tell him, George. Tell him what you did."

"There's nothin' to tell really," he repeated, sounding more than just a little bit irritated. "It was just stupid."

"Tell him, George," Sarah insisted. "If you're not gonna tell him, I'm gonna tell him."

"It's nothin' really. I was drinkin' at *Valley Forge*, up there around the corner on Main Street. I drink there every now and then. . . ￼

"Sarah interrupted him: "About five nights a week."

George continued: "Well, it was gettin' up there near closing time and Billy Abrams, he's the bartender, he takes the cash drawer out of the register and puts it on the bar and starts to count the money. You know, figuring the proceeds for the day. Well, the phone rings and Billy, he goes to the other end of the bar to answer it. Leaves the cash drawer right there on the bar. So when Billy's on the phone, I get up, grab the drawer with the loot in it and walk out the door."

"Just like that?" I asked.

"Yup, right out the door."

When it appeared her boyfriend was going to let the story end right there, Sarah interjected: "So Billy, who Big George knows very well because he drinks at *Valley Forge* so often, he calls the cops and tells them Big George Sullivan stole the cash drawer. And he tells them where Big George lives, right on the corner of Green Street and Warren Avenue."

I got the remainder of the story in bits and pieces from both Big George and Sarah, one then the other. It seems the cops responded to the corner of Green Street and Warren Avenue, hoping to have a word or two with Big George and what do they see? They see Big George sitting on the dead grass in front of the apartment house with the cash drawer on his lap . . . counting the money from the drawer!

I couldn't help but chuckle a little bit when Sarah described that and I theorized that George couldn't be in all that much trouble – certainly he couldn't be facing time behind bars – because the whole ordeal didn't sound like all that much of an infraction.

"What were you charged with, larceny?" I asked.

"Yeah, larceny of more than a hundred dollars," he responded.

"How much money was in the drawer?" I asked.

"I don't know, I didn't do that much counting before the cops came," he responded.

"Well you can't be in that much trouble," I said. "It doesn't sound like very serious shit. Where are you being tried, in the District Court?"

"Yeah, Tuesday in District Court."

"Shit, it's a misdemeanor, no big deal."

"It *is* a big deal," Sarah insisted.

"No, it ain't," George said. "But I've been in trouble before. I've been to prison. In fact, I was on probation when it happened. I could be looking at serious time."

I asked George if he had a lawyer.

He responded in a word. Or, rather, less than a word.

"Nah," he said.

I told him he should have a lawyer and he told me he couldn't afford one.

"What's the matter, don't you watch cop shows on television? If you can't afford a lawyer, one will be appointed to you."

"I've had public defenders before," George spat. "They ain't no good."

I told him I'd get him a lawyer; I'd get him the best lawyer in Massachusetts. I'd get him Kevin Reddington.

"Yeah, I've heard of him," Sarah said.

"I have too," George agreed.

Despite the fact that both Sarah and Big George knew Reddington, at least by reputation, I gave them a rundown of his resume anyway. I told them how he currently had a streak of five acquittals in first-degree murder cases, one case more difficult than the previous one.

"Hey, one of his clients, a broad, walked up the stairs to her second-floor bedroom where her live-in boyfriend was sleeping," I said. "She's got two butcher knives, one in each hand. Real quiet like, she gets up on her bed, so she's kneeling over her boyfriend's head. And then she plunges the knives, one each into both of her old man's eyes.

"Kevin got a not-guilty verdict, claiming battered woman syndrome. One of the first times it was used successfully in the state. Reddington put his client on the stand to tell jurors how her boyfriend was an animal. How he used to force her and her two kids to have sex orgies with him. Well, after one of those sessions, he fell asleep in the second floor bedroom. She quietly went down to the kitchen and retrieved the knives. She said she plunged them into her boyfriend's eyes because she wanted to be certain she killed him.

"She told jurors she didn't know if she *could* kill him. He had bragged to her that he couldn't die. He was actually a Ninja warrior from the days of yore and had been alive for centuries.

"After the chick did the dastardly deed, she gathered her kids and drove to her mother's house, which was on the other side of town, and telephoned the police. She then met the cops back in front of her apartment house. They climbed the stairs to the second-floor bedroom along with her. On the way up – this is unbelievable - she heard her boyfriend moaning and suddenly knew he was telling the truth – he couldn't be killed. She let out a scream and went running back down the stairs.

"He died in the hospital the next day, though."

"And she was found not guilty?" George asked in amazement.

"Yup. Reddington argued that she was temporarily insane due to battered woman syndrome. And, even if she wasn't insane, it was a case of self-defense and defense of her children."

"Yeah, but he was sleeping!" Big George responded.

"Yup, he was sleeping."

Big George ordered another beer for himself, one for Sarah and a vodka and tonic for me. Freddy Fender was proclaiming he was *Not a Fool Anymore* on the jukebox.

"Then there was this other case. A chick, a drug-dealing broad, was sliced up about 48 times in her apartment. This dude comes running out of the apartment building with blood all over him and holding onto a bloody knife. He jumps into a car and takes off. When the cops respond, they send out one of those all-points bulletins for the car that was spotted leaving the scene. About 45 minutes later, the dude is driving along in West Bridgewater when he sees a cruiser behind him. He leads the cops on a short chase, and then he stops, saying he was up in the broad's apartment, free basing crack with her when he blacks out. The next thing he knows, he's driving in West Bridgewater and sees a cop after him.

"Reddington tells the jury the dude was temporarily insane. But even if he wasn't, there could have been someone else up there killing the drug-dealing broad and his client was just a convenient patsy. The dude never admitted killing her.

"Another not guilty. And this one wasn't even on the basis of temporary insanity. This time, jurors were convinced there actually might have been someone else up there carving up the broad and it might not have been the defendant at all.

"Right after the verdict, I was interviewing Reddington for the paper and he sounded like he had a feeling his client didn't do it all along and the jury's verdict proved him right. He said the cops better go back out now and find the real murderer. If they don't, Reddington said, he'd hire a private investigator to go out and do it. I put that quote in the paper, too.

"During the trial, they showed a video-tape of the dude when he gave his statement to the cops after he gave himself up. They called it his 'confession,' but, like I said, it really wasn't because he never said he did it. But he was crying and telling them how he was coked out for days and having blackouts and how he must have done it and he was all remorseful and everything.

"Jesus Christ, he was found not guilty?" George asked.

"Yup."

Then I added: "A lot of people in the courtroom were saying how the cops should make that video tape available to schools to play for kids and show the horror of drugs. They figured it would scare the shit out of a lot of kids using drugs. As I left the courtroom after the verdict, though, I thought it wouldn't be such a good idea. Not if the kids in the schools were told the pitiful dude in the movie beat the rap."

Just about then, old Freddy Fender was telling the world what was going to happen *Before the Next Teardrop Falls.*

"Yeah, OK, so you can get Kevin Reddington to defend me and he's a goddamn miracle worker and he'll get me a not guilty, but how the hell am I going to pay him?" George asked.

"Wow! Wait a minute, I didn't promise you he'd get you a not guilty! That sounds like a pretty difficult thing to do when the police pull up and you're sitting on the grass counting the money you're accused of stealing from a joint's cash drawer. I'm just saying you'll do a helluva lot better with Reddington defending you than you will without Reddington defending you."

"How they hell am I gonna pay him?"

"I'll just tell him you'll pay him what you can when you can, that's all."

In my heart of hearts, I knew Big George was interpreting that as saying he didn't have to pay Kevin any money at all and I figured I'd tell Kevin that's the way George would interpret it. But Kevin and I were really close and I figured that would be OK with him.

"Really?" Bill asked. "Just pay him what I can when I can?"

"Really."

"And he's gonna go along with that bullshit?"

"He's a good friend."

"OK, get me Reddington."

After another drink or two, my prospects at *The Mission* didn't seem all that great. I mean, George was there with Sarah so I knew for certain I wouldn't be going back to my room with her and some of the other broads I had spotted on previous occasions just weren't around that particular night. So I decided to bid goodnight to Big George and Sarah, hop in my automobile and head on over to *Capeway*. Yeah, I thought maybe . . . just maybe . . . I might once again see the goddess with the heavily made up eyes and maybe . . . just maybe . . . I wouldn't wait as long this time and I'd go home with her.

So I drove on over to *Capeway*.

And immediately spotted the dark-haired, dark-eyed goddess . . .

. . . Walking out of *Capeway* with another guy.

He was tall and dark and not the slightest bit handsome.

Well, I say he wasn't the slightest bit handsome, but what the hell do I know from handsome? I don't have any idea what chicks find handsome. Hey, remember, this was 1976. I guess Paul Newman was the heartthrob in '76. I never thought of Paul Newman as being tremendously handsome. And, anyway, this particular dude, I thought to myself, he's no Paul Newman!

As they walked out, the goddess and I made eye contact. We looked through one another. I was positive she remembered me from our long-distance flirting the week before. It was magnetic. If tall, dark and not-so-handsome hadn't been with her, we would have automatically been drawn to one another right then and there. But they passed. And I passed. And that was that!

CHAPTER 15

SPELLBOUND

Two days later, the cold streak had snapped, the calendar noted it was the end of April and spring was in the air. And there was a spring in my step as I exited the elevator at the third-floor city room at *The Examiner*. My progress was stopped by the gruff, growling voice of Managing Editor Hugh Beckerman.

"Scarpati!"

I turned on my heels and headed for his tiny, glassed-in cubicle. That's right, the managing editor didn't have an office, just a cubicle. Shit, 6:23 in the morning and his breath reeked of alcohol. I wondered if mine did, too.

"You're late; where the hell you been?" Beckerman barked.

Refusing to be intimidated, I told him I stopped on my way into work for a massage.

"I'm taking you off the desk this week," he said. "We've got a new girl starting today. She's going to be covering District Court. You've spent time covering that beat. I want you to take her over to the courthouse and show her the ropes. Introduce her around. Then you'll be back on the desk next week."

I glanced over at the desk next to the wire editor, where I would normally be seated, and confirmed for myself that yes, indeed, somebody else was handling page two; my usual task at this hour in the morning. The column I wrote for the editorial page was totally separate and apart from the daily duties.

"So she'll be in at 8," Beckerman growled. "I'll introduce you to her then."

"And what do you want me to do between now and then?"

Beckerman grimaced with the gusto only Beckerman could manage.

"I don't know; go get yourself another massage," he barked.

"I think I'll settle for breakfast," I responded.

I left *The Examiner* and headed for *The Greasy Spoon*. No eggs over easy this time, though. No sausage. I drank a cup of coffee. Regular. And then a couple of refills.

"Scarpati!" Beckerman barked again when I returned to the newsroom at 8:20. "Can't you ever be anywhere on time?"

There was no clever comeback from me this time. Out of the corner of my eye, I spotted a new face several desks down in a row of reporters. And I was spellbound.

"Come with me," Beckerman growled as he got up from his desk and walked past me. I followed in his tracks. Straight to the *Capeway* goddess. Her dark black hair still shined with a hint of blue. And she was still overly made up. But she was beautiful. She wasn't clad as seductively as she was the first two times I had seen her, she was dressed far more appropriately for the office. But she'd be stunning in anything.

"Well, hello!" I exclaimed as Beckerman and I approached.

I guess Beckerman caught the familiar infliction in my voice.

"You two know each other?" he asked.

To my ultimate consternation, the young goddess merely looked baffled.

"We don't really *know* each other," I responded. We saw each other at *Capeway* last week . . . and then again, briefly, Saturday night."

Sounding embarrassed, the goddess hesitated and then said, weakly: "I . . . don't . . . really recall."

"You were at *Capeway* the past two Saturday nights?" I challenged.

"Yes, I was there," she responded weakly.

"Well, I guess the young lady here made more of an impression on you than you did on her," Beckerman chimed in. "And I can certainly appreciate why. Rocky, I want you to meet Audacity Monroe . . . Audacity, Rocky here, is going to walk you over to the District Courthouse and show you the ropes, introduce you around. He'll be with you for a week."

With that, Beckerman wheeled around on his heels and headed back for his cubicle, leaving me with the raving beauty.

"Audacity, unusual name," I observed, "what kind of name is that?"

"Audacity – boldness, daring, fearlessness, insolence, effrontery," she responded as if she were reading from a dictionary. A stock answer to a question that is often asked of her, I figured.

"You left out rude," I told her.

Nothing from the young lady at the moment.

"Audacity, can't it also mean rude?"

Just a hint of a smile from the goddess.

"Oh, am I being rude?"

I didn't respond.

"Touché," I guess it could," she conceded.

"You know, what I was actually asking is how you got the name. Is it ethnic?"

"No, not that I know of. My grandmother's name was Audacity and my father named me after her."

"Your father did, as opposed to your parents?"

"That's right, my mom denies any responsibility for it."

"Your father should have named you Marilyn," I suggested. When she didn't respond, I added: "then you'd be Marilyn Monroe."

"I'm not blonde," she said.

"Very true. But you are stunning. Very beautiful."

"Flattery will get you anywhere," she chided.

"We'll see about that," I said.

"Well almost anywhere," she retorted.

After a while, Audacity and I walked over to the District Courthouse on West Elm Street. As we walked, I asked her if she had been telling the truth, if she really hadn't remembered seeing me at *Capeway*.

"Sorry," she said. "I don't mean to hurt your feelings."

I asked her who the dude was that she left the lounge with two nights before.

"Just someone I left the lounge with," she responded.

We arrived at the courthouse and, as I introduced her, several aspects of our previous conversation were repeated. You know, the one about the origin of her name and how she happened to get it. And then – oh, shit! – we ran into Kevin Reddington in the afternoon. It was a lucky thing that we did. I hadn't given a second thought about the promise I made to Big George a couple of nights before and he was due in that very same courthouse the next day.

We met Kevin in the Green Room. At least I call it the Green Room. That was due to my theatrical training. Did I mention to you I was a theatrical-school dropout? Anyhow, in a theatre, the Green Room is where cast members hang out when they're not on stage. It's where they drink their coffee and chat about the events of the day and what's happening on Broadway. And smoke. At least you could back then. This was back in the days when there were places you could smoke in public buildings. Well, the Brockton District Court has this room – I suppose all courthouses have those rooms – where attorneys drink their coffee, chat about the events of the day and what's happening in the Supreme Court. And, yeah, you could smoke there, too. I guess you could call it a conference room because there is, indeed, a conference table in there. And lawyers have been known to, from time to time; confer with their clients at that very table. But I referred to it as the Green Room.

Anyhow, Audacity and I came upon Kevin sitting there, drinking coffee and dispensing advice to a young public defender who was outraged about a motion that didn't go his way earlier in the day. Audacity and I waited for Kevin to conclude his unofficial seminar and then we approached him. I introduced them and Kevin told her she was much too beautiful to be hanging around with a punch-drunk prize fighter.

"You're a prize fighter?" Audacity asked me in amazement.

"Not any more . . . I'll tell you about it sometime."

I asked Kevin if we could step outside into the corridor. I had something I wanted to ask him about privately.

I told him a good friend had gotten into some trouble. Then I corrected myself and said, "Well, he's not actually a good friend; he's the building manager in the joint where I'm living." I told him *my friend* had gotten himself into a jam, though, and I'd be highly indebted to him if he'd help Big George out of it.

"Sure, anything for you," Kevin smiled.

I gave Kevin a brief rundown of George's predicament, which resulted in a little more than a minor chuckle from Kevin.

"Kevin, I don't know what he's going to be able to pay you."

"Don't worry about it. This one will be on the house," he responded.

"Well, I told him to pay you what he can when he can. Knowing George, though, that may turn out to be *on the house* anyway."

"Gotcha!"

"When is he due in court?" Kevin asked.

"Tomorrow."

"Hmmm. I have to be in Superior Court first thing in the morning," Kevin said. "Tell George to tell the judge he has a lawyer, his lawyer hasn't arrived yet and to hold the case for second call."

After work that day, I stopped on the first floor of the rooming house, to knock on Big George's door.

Sarah answered it. A sparkle in her eye.

"To what do I owe this pleasant surprise?" she asked in her down-home accent.

I asked to see George, but Sarah said he wasn't in.

103

"I'd invite you in, but I don't know how long it will be before he gets home," she said.

I told her to deliver Kevin Reddington's message and she said that she would.

Later that night, just about the time I had closed my eyes in earnest and was on the doorway to sleep, there was a knock on my door. It was Sarah's knock. One knock, then a pause and then another knock. Then quick three knocks consecutively. Yup, it was Sarah's knock. I knew it was her because she was the only person – ever – who knocked on my second-floor Green street door.

I didn't respond.

She knocked again.

Slightly harder.

Same sequence.

I still didn't respond.

Five minutes passed.

I heard a key in my door.

I heard the tumblers in the lock fall.

Is that what tumblers do in a lock?

They fall?

Anyway, I heard them do whatever tumblers do.

The door opened.

Sarah stepped inside.

"I'm not here to fool around; I'm just here to sleep."

A thousand questions rushed through my mind.

Did George and Sarah have a fight? Where was he, anyway, out again . . . somewhere getting laid? Home? Did they have words? More than words?

Yeah, a thousand questions rushed through my mind.

But I didn't ask any of them.

"Why didn't you answer the door when I knocked?" she answered.

"When? When did you knock?"

"Just a few minutes ago."

"I didn't hear you. I must have been asleep."

Sarah stripped and lay down next to me.

As I laid there – shortly before I drifted off to sleep – one thing became abundantly clear: If there's one thing that will piss you off more than a chick knocking on your door in the middle of the night for sex; it's a chick knocking on the door in the middle of the night *not* for sex.

CHAPTER 16

THE SUNNY SIDE OF P.T. BARNUM

Striking.

Most definitely striking!

Sure, she wore too much makeup.

Too much lipstick.

She almost looked clownish.

But goddamn beautiful.

The sunny side of P.T. Barnum.

Whatever that means.

I felt like holding Audacity's hand as we walked over to the District Courthouse the next morning. But I didn't.

"Tell me the truth; did you really not remember me from *Capeway* those two Saturday nights?

"I'm sorry. I didn't. I don't. It really bothers you, doesn't it?

"I guess so. I was sort of spellbound myself. I thought it was mutual."

"If you were so spellbound, why didn't you approach me?"

Right then and there, some kind of yellow hot-rod convertible came by us with its radio blaring. It diverted our attention so I didn't have to respond to Audacity's question, which was a very good thing because I had no idea what I was going to offer for a response.

You'd think Big George would have dressed a little bit for his appearance in court. He was clad in dungarees – at least they looked

107

fairly new and relatively clean – but he was also sporting a t-shirt – a white t-shirt. I never would have anticipated George putting on a dress shirt and tie for court. But hell at least a sports shirt with a collar would have been better. Or, if he were so damned determined to wear a t-shirt, you'd think it would be a colored t-shirt. But, there he was in a white t-shirt that could probably be mistaken for a gray t-shirt because it obviously hadn't been washed in the current calendar year.

"George Sullivan."

The clerk called his name and George, in all his understated glory, appeared at the railing that separated the spectators from the court principals.

"Mr. Sullivan, are you represented by counsel?" Judge George Coventry, a little guy with a red face and a pencil-thin moustache inquired.

"What?"

"Do you have a lawyer?"

"Yeah, I got a lawyer."

"And who is it that's representing you?"

"Kevin Reddington."

"And where is Mr. Reddington?"

"I don't know; he's not here," George stated the obvious.

"Well, we'll hold your case over to second call to give Mr. Reddington an opportunity to appear."

"No, that's OK; you don't gotta do that."

"Well, what would you have me do?"

"I'll just plead guilty and get the whole thing over with."

I felt like jumping to my feet and shouting at George: "What the hell are you doing?" But I didn't.

"Do you want to spend time behind bars, Mr. Sullivan?" the judge blared and not happily.

George merely shrugged his shoulders and mumbled something that was inaudible.

Directing his remark toward a court officer now, the judge barked, "Teddy, show Mr. Sullivan our accommodations! Escort him to lockup!"

The officer stepped forward, clasped Big George's elbow and shoved him toward the door.

A good 20 minutes later, Kevin Reddington appeared in the courtroom. The judge immediately summoned him: "Mr. Reddington."

Kevin approached, swung the railing gate open and entered the battle field.

"Good morning, judge," he acknowledged.

"Good morning, Mr. Reddington."

"I'm sorry for being late," Kevin apologized. "I had a conference in the Superior Courthouse. It was a command performance."

"Well, I sent a client of yours to lockup," the judge noted. "It was a Mister . . . Mister . . . what was his name?"

"The question was directed to the court clerk.

The clerk shuffled papers and responded: "It was a Mr. . . . Mr. Sullivan."

"Sullivan?" Kevin repeated, sounding confused.

"I couldn't stay moot any longer."

"Kevin . . . Big George," I spoke up in a semi-hushed tone.

"Oh, yeah, Big George Sullivan!" he exclaimed.

"Well . . . yes, he was rather massive," Coventry agreed.

"He came into court offering to plead guilty. He said he wanted to get the whole thing over with. I sent him to lockup to cool his heels."

"I'll have a chat with him there," Kevin suggested.

"Fine, we'll put Mr. Sullivan's case on for second call."

When Reddington and George returned to the courtroom and the case was called again, the judge commented: "I believe we had an offer of a change of plea."

"Why would he do that, Your Honor; he's not guilty?" Kevin retorted.

"Then let's set a date for trial," Coventry said.

Each day – Monday through Thursday – Audacity and I returned to The Examiner to chronicle the happenings of the day in the District Courthouse. And all four days, I suggested we grab a bite to eat for dinner and all four nights she turned me down. Each time with a different excuse.

Sufficiently depressed by Audacity's rejections, I went out Thursday night and drank the night fantastic. I did quite a bit of that in and around that point in my life. If I got depressed, which happened fairly regularly, I drank.

When anything went particularly well and I was feeling good – which wasn't all that often – I drank to celebrate. But then, quite often, I drank merely to pass the time.

This particular Thursday night, the next day being a work day and all, I drank hard, but did the responsible thing and returned to my room before midnight. I drifted off to dreamland somewhere around midnight. Just about the time I was leaving the state of consciousness, I heard a gentle rap, rap, rap on my door. I didn't want to be bothered. Besides I thought Sarah had a nerve to assume she could just drop in at any hour during the night whenever she felt like it. Rap! Rap! Rap! A more sturdy knock this time. But I continued to ignore her.

Based on a previous "visit" when the knocking ceased and was followed by silence, I knew she had retreated to the first floor to get the spare key to my room. So, I flipped the sliding bolt on the inside of my door.

Sure enough, minutes later I heard the lock turn over. The outside of the door, by the way, was the only place for a key. Sarah was probably pretty pissed when she discovered I had bolted the door on the inside and she couldn't get in.

It was a rude awakening when my alarm blared at 6 o'clock in the morning. I pulled on a pair of pants and grabbed a bar of soap and shampoo to hustle down the hall to the common bathroom for a quick shower; only to be rejected when I flipped the bolt to open the door. It didn't budge. Goddamn it, Sarah had left it locked from the outside. And there was no key hole for me to unlock it on the inside.

The first thing I did was hurry to my front window to survey the situation. A tree, very nearby. Could I climb out of the window onto the tree and down to the ground. Hell, no, I'm no monkey; they're a lot more coordinated than I am. I'd end up on the ground alright. On my back!

Hurriedly, I got dressed for work. Suit. Shirt and tie. Spit-shined shoes. Hell, who am I kidding? I never spit-shined a thing in my life.

Then I banged on the wall to awake a dude in the next room. I had never met him. Had never even spoken to him. Nice time to introduce myself, huh?

On about the 18th knock, I heard a very weary, somewhat inquisitive, somewhat bullshit voice from beyond the wall.

"Yeah?"

"Hey, I'm really sorry. But I got a problem!

"I gotta get to work, but, damnit, I'm locked in my room!"

"How the hell did you do that?"

"I don't have the faintest idea. But I gotta get to work. Will you go get Big George and have him come up with a key to get me out?"

"How the hell did you do that? How'd you lock yourself in?"

"I told you; I don't have the slightest idea. Will you get George?"

"Yeah, hold your horses. I'll get him!"

Then silence.

For quite a long time.

I knocked on the wall again in case my neighbor had fallen back to sleep.

Nothing.

Then, finally, I heard a key in the door. It swung open.

"How the hell did this happen?" George questioned.

I considered telling him his beloved girlfriend did it.

Yeah, I considered telling him, but I decided discretion would be, in this instance, the better part of valor.

"I don't know," I said, "I don't have the slightest idea."

111

So George let me out without the benefit of an explanation and I actually arrived at work 10 minutes early that particular day.

Jump ahead one week – exactly one week, the following Friday – I was meandering along the hallway to that famous common bathroom and I heard George and Sarah screaming at one another from their room below.

"I know you're screwing someone in the building," George bellowed. "Who the hell is it?"

"Don't tell him, Sarah," I whispered to myself. "Don't tell him." I said it out loud.

I probably should have been more than a little bit nervous about how Sarah was going to respond to Big George's question. George, I had learned, was known far and wide as a very tough guy. I had also heard that he packed a gun. Yeah, I should have been worried, but I wasn't. Maybe it was because I had done Big George a tremendous favor by fixing him up with Kevin Reddington. That should count for something. In the heat of the moment, George probably wouldn't even think about my getting him an attorney. Not any attorney, but the best in the great Commonwealth of Massachusetts.

"Who the hell are you screwing?" George screamed.

I didn't hear Sarah's respond. It was muffled. But I didn't think she gave me up. And, I didn't hear from George that night either.

CHAPTER 17

NEVER DID CARE MUCH FOR FIREWORKS

In case you've gotten the impression that I was pretty depressed at this point in my life, you certainly got that right. I was at *The Mission*, sipping vodka and tonics, chain smoking cigarettes and remembering how absolutely wonderful the previous Thanksgiving and New Year's Day had been. Spending them in bed with Barbara – drinking, snorting coke and making love. Spending a holiday in bed may not sound like the most exquisite formula for an enjoyable holiday to you, but that's because you've never made love to Barbara.

I'm not certain why I had meandered over to *the Mission*. Was I hoping to run into Sarah and hook up with her again? Since all that shit happened a couple of months before, Sarah had stopped coming around. I'm not really sure I cared – might even have been thankful for it – but here I was dropping into *The Mission* on the Fourth of July. Shortly after my arrival, someone told me Big George and Sarah had gone away for the holiday. I hadn't even asked. Someone just volunteered it. A few guys I knew from the streets came in and I started drinking with them. One was Bobby the Car Thief. I started drinking with him and a few other dudes whose names I didn't even know. But I had seen them here and there from time to time.

We began drinking tequila and buying one another shots. Drinking tequila was never one of my more favorite things to do because I always – always – got sick any time I drank it. But I drank. And drank. More to be social than anything.

I was happy as hell that all this happened at a gin joint so close to my rooming house and my car was parked safely away on Green Street because I knew damn well, I was in no condition to drive. Damn, I was drunk. Dizzy and drunk.

I walked through the wooded area between *The Mission* and Green Street – the route Sarah had taught me.

As I staggered up the stairs to the front door at 113 Green Street, I was hit by a wave. A wave of nausea. I was trying to be so fast inserting my key into the front door lock, I missed it about four times. Damn, unlocking a door can be a near impossible task when you're dead drunk and nauseated as all hell.

Once inside, I scampered up the stairs to the second floor. Scampered? Hell, no! I stumbled up the stairs in a hurry. All the time praying that nobody would be using the john at the end of the second-floor hallway. Nobody was. I threw open the door and almost made it to the toilet when the vomit let go. I didn't attempt to clean it. I was too drunk to really care. Besides, that would be up to Big George to do the cleaning. He was, after all, the building manager.

Looking back on the whole misadventure, I suppose that was one way to spend the Fourth of July. I never did care that much for fireworks, anyway.

CHAPTER 18

MEETING ON THE BOULE ... THE AVENUE

I guess by now you're convinced that I spent as little time as possible in my second-floor room on Green Street. Just too damn depressing. But this particular night I grabbed hold of the novel THE CATCHER IN THE RYE by J.D. Salinger. It is probably my favorite book. I've read it about a dozen times. I've got to admit, there were several periods in my life that Holden Caulfield was a hero of mine. I always told myself if I ever got a kitty, I'd make sure it was a female and I'd name her Phoebe, after Holden Caulfield's sister.

I opened CATCHER and a card that I had been using as a bookmark fell out.

I smiled when I thought about it.

Call it a fluke.

A chance meeting.

Or call it fate.

I had been strolling along the main drag at Nantasket Beach. The very beautiful beach on one side of me. Paragon Park, an amusement park with one of the largest wooden roller coasters of all time on the other side. I have no idea what brought me there that particular night. Maybe it was the bright lights. Maybe it was the scent of booze emanating from Mike Burns Inn that caught my nose and my imagination and dragged me along. But, yup, it was probably fate.

I was dressed appropriately for the humid night and the locale, wearing dungarees, a tank top and sandals. Approaching from the opposite direction was a young lady – a blonde bombshell decked out in flaming pink.

Flaming pink?

What the hell is flaming pink anyway?

A combination of bright red and yellow most certainly is flaming. But pink?

Nope.

This beautiful woman, the blonde chick, was wearing passionate pink.

That' right. Pink can't be flaming, but it most definitely can be passionate.

Aside from the passionate pink dress and coat, the chick was wearing a very wide-brimmed hat, a bright, multi-colored scarf and heels; bright yellow heels. And very large, domineering dark glasses. It was twilight. She obvious didn't need the glasses to deflect the light. But her outfit would not be complete if she hadn't been wearing them.

She walked right up to me – smiling – winked and handed me her card. Of course there was no way I could see her wink with the shades she was wearing. I'm just certain that she did. . . she winked!

"Call me sometime," she said in the most sensuous voice she – or anyone this side of Broadway – could muster.

"I don't even know your name."

"It's on the card," she responded.

"You don't know my name."

"You'll tell me when you call."

Now – I guess it was weeks later – the card fell out of THE CATCHER IN THE RYE and onto my bed.

I picked it up and wondered why I hadn't called the number on it before now.

And decided it was time.

I had to leave my rooming house and walk down Green Street and cross Main to *The Examiner* to make the call. I had no telephone in my room. That was a luxury I was learning to live without.

"Hello, Fredrica?" I asked when she answered the phone.

"My friends call me Ricki."

"Your card says it's Fredrica."

"My friends call me Ricki."

"OK, Ricki. . . you don't know me."

"I'll have to take your word for that . . . since you haven't told me who's calling."

"My name's Rocky, Rocky Scarpati."

"Well, hello, Rocky Scarpati. To what do I owe this pleasure?"

"You probably don't remember me, but I was strolling along Nantasket Boulevard, minding my own business a couple of weeks ago when you approached me, handed me your card and told me to call you sometime."

"That's not true," she said.

"Certainly, it is."

"No, I wouldn't have given you my card on Nantasket Boulevard," she said, "because Nantasket Boulevard doesn't exist. I might have given you my card on Nantasket Avenue, which certainly is busy and festive enough to be a boulevard, but it's an avenue."

"Well, you did; you gave me your card on the avenue, so I'm calling you. You probably don't remember me."

"I don't know; do you smoke a pipe?"

"No."

"Then you're probably the guy with the pink earring."

"I've been known to wear a pink earring every now and then."

"So that was you, the gentleman with the pink earring."

It had been a while since anyone had referred to me as *a gentleman*.

"I'm surprised you remember me."

"Hey, don't think I run around giving out my card to any Tom, Dick or Harry," Ricki protested. "In fact, that was the only time I can remember ever doing it."

There was a bit of an uncomfortable silence right about there.

"So I'm wondering if maybe you'd like to go out to dinner."

"That depends."

"Depends on what?"

"On where you're going to take me for dinner."

"Where would you like me to take you for dinner?"

"Melio's . . . in Norton."

"Why Melio's?"

"I know the owner, Hank Tartaglia. He's a good guy. I try to get there every now and then, but I haven't been in quite a long time."

"Hank Tartaglia an old boyfriend?"

"No, nothing like that. Just a friend."

"OK, Melio's it is. Saturday night?"

"Yes, OK."

"How do you know I'm not a serial rapist."

"No serial rapist worth his salt would ever wear pink earrings."

Hank, a little guy with tightly-cropped curly hair and a smile as wide as the Brooklyn Bridge, appeared happy to see Ricki when we arrived at Melio's Saturday night.

But, to be perfectly frank, I think he seemed happier to see me.

"You didn't tell me you knew Hank Tartaglia," Ricki commented.

"You didn't ask; Hank and I go way back," I responded.

"Way back," Hank agreed.

"I didn't know you two were an item," he noted.

"Not an item,' I said, "Ricki just recently picked me up on Nantasket Bouli. . . Nantasket Avenue."

"Hold on, I've got a very special table I want to sit you at, but there's a couple seated there right now. They're just about to pay their bill, so I'll hustle them out of here, we'll clear the table and I'll have you seated in five minutes, 10 at the most."

The table Hank had promised was in the very center of the floor. It had an unobstructed view of a painting on the wall directly across from it. A table which would have been right next to the painting had been removed to give the artwork the viewing space it so richly deserved.

When we were seated at the table – obviously reserved for the elite – Hank sat down to join us.

"You shouldn't have given the couple who were seated here the bum's rush," I said to Hank. "We've got all night. We could have waited."

"I don't think they minded at all," Hank replied. "I told them we had some very special people coming in to sit at this very special table and informed them their meals were on the house if they could get out in five minutes. Believe me; they had no problem leaving."

Then Hank half turned to the wall featuring the painting, waved his arm out grandly toward it and remarked: "There you have it!"

It was a painting of Brockton Massachusetts' most famous son, Rocky Marciano, landing his legendary right hand to the side of the head of Jersey Joe Walcott, to win the most coveted title in all of sports; boxing's heavyweight championship of the world. That was on September 23, 1952.

Being a former pugilist myself and hailing from the city of Brockton, I obviously needed no explanation of what I was seeing. But I relayed the info to Ricki on the chance that she wasn't a fan of the manly art.

"Rocky's brother, Peter, was in a while ago and he absolutely fell in love with the painting," Hank said. "So I hired an artist to make a copy of it and I'm going to be presenting it to Peter. I'm having a little party, a gala event, Wednesday night to present it to Peter. I'd like the two of you to be here as my guests."

"We'd love to come," I responded. "Well, there I go again, being too sure of myself." I turned to Ricki and said: "I'd love to come to

Hank's party. But I can't speak for you. Would you like to be my date?"

This from Ricki: "I think I probably would. But, of course, it depends on how the remainder of tonight goes."

"We'll be here," I told Hank.

"Hey, I just had a thought. Any chance you could write about it afterward. You know, put it in your column."

"Oh, so there was a method to your madness, an ulterior motive. But I certainly believe there is every chance in the world of our attending. I'll even get a photographer here to dress up the column."

It most certainly was a gala affair the following Saturday night. Hank had invited – I don't know – a dozen or maybe 15 individuals to enjoy the festivities when he uncovered and presented the painting to Peter. To coin a phrase, a good time was had by all.

The Enterprise editors moved my column off the editorial page – put it on the first page, second section- so that they could give the column the kind of splurge it so richly deserved. My column this particular week was accompanied by a half dozen photos.

I should mention, after the gala, Ricki invited me to her place. Our date came to an abrupt end when Ricki laid a right hook on me that was reminiscent of the right hand Rocky landed on Walcott in the painting. I'm not going to say that Ricki's assault was totally without justification. But I'm not going to say it *was* justified, either.

CHAPTER 19

DINNER CONVERSATION

The spectacular layout in the newspaper appeared in Wednesday's edition. Friday, I received a telephone call at the office from Hank telling me I had to – I simply had to – come to Melio's for dinner Saturday night. He had something he had to – he simply had to – tell me.

We were seated at the same table we occupied the first time I gazed upon the brilliant Marciano-Walcott painting on the restaurant wall. It took me about two-thirds of a moment to realize the artwork was no longer there.

"You're not gonna believe what happened after you printed that story Wednesday night!" Hank exclaimed, the smile on his face as broad as the George Washington Bridge. "First I gotta give you a little background.

"The painting originally came from my cousin Sal. It was in his garage. I got no idea how long it was in his garage, but he recently found it there and he thought it would look great in the restaurant. So he gave it to me or loaned it to me or whatever it was he did.

"So, then like you already know, Peter Marciano came in and fell in love with the painting. So I hired an artist to copy the painting and presented it to Peter. You were here, you wrote about it. Very good story, by the way."

Then, without skipping a beat, Hank said, "Who is this with you, by the way? I thought you were bringing Ricki. I never saw you with this young lady before?"

"Well, Hank, you have quite the audacity, asking who I'm with. This beautiful young lady happens to be named Audacity."

"Nice to meet you," Hank said to Audacity.

Then he continued: "We made a very big deal about presenting the copy of the painting to Peter. Everybody was here. Everybody except my cousin, Salvatore. Well, Sal, who they call Slippery Sal at the sanitation department where he works. . ."

"Wait a minute," I interrupted. "What do they call him?"

"Slippery Sal. That's what they call him."

"So, anyway, when he saw your story in the newspaper, he got a hair across his ass. I guess he was bullshit because he didn't get invited to the dinner or because his name wasn't in the paper or 'cause his picture wasn't in the paper; I don't know, but he got bullshit!

"So the next night, Thursday night, he comes into the restaurant during the peak dinner hour and takes the painting off the wall. He said it was a loan and he's takin' it back."

I loved it. Great follow-up column.

The following Wednesday, I told the world how Salvatore Tartaglia, aka Slippery Sal of the Brockton Sanitation Department, angered because his picture wasn't in the paper, marched into his cousin's restaurant during the peak dinner hour, hoisted the painting off the wall and carried it away."

I theorized that it made tremendous dinner conversation for the dozens of patrons on hand at Melio's.

Later, after that, my bosses and I received notification from the court that Sliipery Sal had filed suit against the newspaper and me, claiming that I had tarnished his reputation.

Cute.

Slippery Sal didn't stand a chance. The attorney *The Examiner* had hired to defend both the newspaper and Yours Truly, filed a motion to have it thrown out of court. My good friend, Judge Augustus F. Wagner, sitting in criminal court, saw the motion was a scheduled to be heard before a judge in the civil court. Gus arranged for the motion to be transferred to the criminal courtroom before him. Later that day I got a call at the newspaper.

"Rocky?"

"Yup."

"This is Gus Wagner."

"Well, hello!" I exclaimed, surprised to hear from him. He had never called before.

"There was a motion before me today by your attorney to dismiss Salvatore Tartaglia's suit against you. I just wanted to let you know that I read the column when it was put into evidence. Good humor."

After the call, I went to see William J. Casey. I told the managing editor not to worry about Slipper Sal's lawsuit. I was certain it hadn't survived its day in court.

CHAPTER 20

HOW AM I DRIVING?

Shortly after Slippery Sal's repossession of the Marciano painting, Peter Mallory, a truck driver at *The Examiner*, cornered me in a corridor at the newspaper and barked: "What are you doing about the new signs they're going to put on the back of the trucks?"

I was president of the union that represented journalists, advertising people, the business office, the maintenance department and truck drivers at the newspaper.

Blake Richardson, a truck driver, had been president of the union – The Brockton Media Guild – when I went to work there. He had been at the helm of the Brockton Guild for several years and was an effective union president until he suddenly announced he wasn't running for re-election. A few months after he made that statement, Richardson was proclaimed manager of the Circulation Department. That's when Blake's decision not to seek another term as union president became crystal clear. His promotion into management, for all intents and purposes, must have been a done deal.

In any event, Blake Richardson's departure from the union ranks left a void. I decided to run for president. To be perfectly honest, there didn't appear to be anyone else remotely qualified who was chomping at the bit to assume the role and I was pretty well known throughout the Brockton local and was generally considered to be a pretty good union man although maybe a little bit of a thug. I had been arrested twice on picket lines – once in Brockton and once in Providence, R.I. – and like I mentioned before, in Providence I had actually been arrested and went to trial in connection with the murder of the leader of another union that was scabbing there. But, hey, I was found not guilty of that crime.

I had another reason for running for union president. It was in my blood. My dad, Tony Scarpati, was a union activist in the bus drivers' union.

So I announced my candidacy to run for president of the Brockton Media Guild and nobody ran against me. And, now, here was Peter Mallory, asking about new signs on the backs of delivery trucks; signs I knew nothing about!

"What are you talking about, what signs?" I asked Mallory.

"The signs Richardson intends to put on the rear of the trucks beginning next week. Shit, didn't he even tell you about it? Isn't he supposed to negotiate something like that with you?"

"Yeah, I suppose he should have. But, you know as well as I do, Peter, Blake doesn't always do what he's supposed to do."

Several prior union presidents were promoted into management at *The Examiner*. I can understand why being the head of a union could be a pathway into management. When you're the chief union dude you certainly get the attention of business owners and their managers. For better or worse. You have the opportunity to show them how effective you can be. And creative.

I've come to learn that there are two ways union officials can go into management. You can remain a good union man at heart. You can remember where you came from and treat the people who work for you fairly. Or not.

So, right now, Blake Richardson was the circulation department manager and I was president of the union. And here was truck driver Peter Mallory asking me what the hell was going on with the signs that I didn't have any idea about. Peter Mallory was a tall, read-headed dude who was well endowed with acne scars from when he was a kid. He had extra thick eye lashes and a set of teeth, which were too large for his mouth, which was quite strange because his mouth was overly large in itself. His irritating voice resembled an itch that can't be scratched. Despite all these shortcomings, however, Mallory had an ego the size of San Antonio and he was more than a little quick on the draw to criticize me as union president. I'm certain he felt ultimately more confident to do the job and probably wished beyond belief that he was heading our union.

"Starting next Monday, there's going to be signs on the backs of the trucks. HOW AM I DRIVING?' Then they're going to have a telephone number that people can call if they don't like the way we're driving. What are you gonna do about it?"

"Hey, Peter, I just heard about it. We've got a union meeting tomorrow night. I'll tell you and the rest of the members my battle plan then."

When I got back to my desk, the first thing I did was dial Blake Richardson's number.

"Blake, we need to talk."

"Come on down."

That was easy; so far, so good.

Blake Richardson was a big dude. Looked a lot like John Wayne, but instead of coming across as burly and tough, he actually appeared a bit feminine. He walked with a hint of a sway and talked slightly swishy.

"I hear you're putting signs on the rear of the trucks."

"Yes, that's right."

"Why didn't you tell me about it?"

"Why would I tell you about it?"

"It's a unilateral change in working conditions."

"I don't see why; how does it change anyone's working conditions?"

"If someone calls saying a driver was speeding or cutting someone off or driving like a fool, you'll discipline him. Before the signs, he wouldn't be disciplined because you wouldn't know about it. That's a unilateral change in working conditions. You've got to negotiate it."

"I don't agree," Richardson said. "But, if you want to negotiate, go ahead; let's negotiate."

"OK, I want you to agree that nobody will be disciplined as a result of a negative telephone call."

"I can't agree to that."

To tell you the truth, I never expected that he could.

So I switched gears.

"The telephone number that's going to be listed on the trucks; who's going to be assigned to that."

"Blaze Starr. Any calls will go directly to her. You know Blaze don't you?"

"Yeah, I know her."

Hell, I thought everyone within a fifty-mile radius of Brockton knew her.

"If she's going to be fielding the calls, you're adding to her workload. You've got to negotiate a new salary for her."

"Don't be ridiculous." Richardson blurted with a flourishing wave of his hand. See what I meant about the feminine aspect of Blake? Every now and then, he would wave his hand frivolously or flick his wrist and his words were often delivered in a sing-song tone.

Anyhow, he told me not to be ridiculous. He wasn't going to increase Blaze's salary and he didn't expect those signs would generate any telephone calls in any event.

"They never do." Richardson spat with a certain gusto. "Nobody ever calls those numbers. They're just posted on the rear of the trucks to give the public the impression we're a responsible employer,"

"OK, since nobody ever makes those calls, give her twenty dollars for each one she does receive."

"Jesus Christ, Rocky!" he exclaimed. But then, after a long hesitation as if he were giving it serious thought, Blake said, "OK, I'll give her two dollars a call."

"Give her three," I retorted.

"Two," he insisted.

"If she's not gonna be receiving any calls, what the hell does it matter? Three dollars."

"OK, I'll give her three dollars a call. Goddamn it, Rocky, you drive a hard bargain."

I knew he was simply stroking my ego and didn't mean it.

"I want it in writing," I told Richardson.

"OK, draw it up, I'll sign it."

I know it doesn't sound it – not at all – but I had gotten exactly what I came in for.

CHAPTER 21

KILLING JOSE CERVANTES

"There's one more thing I want to talk to you about . . . Jose Cervantes. I think you're trying to kill him!"

Jose Cervantes was listed on *The Examiner* roster as a district manager – aka truck driver – but for the past six years had been assigned to the shipping room where newspapers were sent after leaving the presses. A large group of part-timers, mostly – if not all – women, put sections of the paper together to make the complete package. A district manager was assigned to oversee the entire process and make sure the correct number of papers went to the right trucks. For the past six years – Monday through Friday – that district manager was Jose Cervantes.

But Jose's wife telephoned me to report that all of that was going to change. She said her husband had been told by *Mr. Richardson* that he was being taken out of the shipping room and would be assigned a truck route. She said Joe was extremely upset by the development.

"He's not a well man," Mrs. Cervantes agonized. "He has a bad heart and he's just trying to hang on until he can retire at 65."

"How old is he now?" I asked.

"He's 63. Please, Mr. Scarpati, help him. He's so very upset about going back out on the road."

"Call me Rocky. I'll see what I can do. I can't promise a thing. Joe's listed as a district manager, which means they can assign him to a truck route. They can require him to manage districts. But I'll see if I can do anything."

"Thank you, thank you, thank you, Mr. Scar . . . Rocky."

Maybe I took the wrong tact with Blake Richardson, coming right out and accusing him of attempting to kill Jose. The John Wayne look-a-like turned beet red in the face and stuttered: "I-I-I resent that a-accusation!"

I had never heard him stutter before.

"He has a heart condition. He's extremely upset and the pressure of being out on the road will kill him."

"Then tell him to retire."

"He's got more than a year before he can do that."

"Then tell him to do the year on the job he was hired for."

Like I told you before – there are two ways a good union man can go into management. He can remain a good union man at heart. He can remember where he came from and treat the people who work for him right.

Or he can be like Blake Richardson.

I just want to be clear about one thing. Sure, there certainly was a history at *The Examiner* of union presidents being promoted into management. That would never happen to me. I was a true blue union man. True blue all the way. I'd never accept a job in management.

If nothing else, my meeting with Blake gave me the perfect opportunity – excuse? - to invite Blaze Starr out for drinks after work. Blaze was a sleek, sexy blonde. Back in the days when I was a young man, my world was filled with beautiful blondes. Everybody knows *GENTLEMEN PREFER BLONDES. Ok, Ok,* I was no gentleman. But I definitely preferred blondes. My first serious girlfriend – a chick by the name of Monica – was a drop-dead gorgeous blonde. The girl – woman? – I married, Susan Razkowski, was a luscious blonde. I don't know if my taste had changed, but as you know, the women more currently in my life were no longer blonde. There was Barbara who I once dearly loved and probably still loved and would forever. But I couldn't be living with her or dating her or having intimate relations for fear I might kill her. There was Eva Green, a total and complete knockout who insisted we couldn't see one another. . . at least until after the Maurice diMontiferro murder trial. Then, of course, there was Audacity Monroe, the chick who may – or may not – have worn too much makeup, but whose unique beauty and tremendous body were overwhelming. I lusted over that one, but as of yet, hadn't gotten into the batter's box, never mind first base. And then came Sarah. But fortunately, my relationship with the big ol' Okie girl was over since the night I locked her out.

Thinking a little bit about Blaze Starr – kind of sounds like a porn star, doesn't it? – I wondered if my fascination with blondes was back, since I invited her out for drinks. The way she dressed simply demanded attention. Extremely provocative.

When Blaze agreed to meet me for drinks, I suggested the lounge at the *Palace Hotel*. I suppose the most convenient place for us to get together would have been *the Ambassador* right behind *The Examiner*. But I wanted to ensure that we could talk without being interrupted by *Examiner* folk. And aside from that, I felt *The Palace Hotel* would be the proper venue if everything between Blaze and myself went really, really well.

Heads turned when she walked into the *Palace Hotel* lounge to meet me. That was nothing new. Heads turned wherever Blaze walked. She didn't have the long flowing blonde hair that so intrigued me when I was young. The long flowing blonde hair of Monica and Susan. No, Blaze's was much shorter. And spiked.

I asked Blaze if she was aware of the pending *HOW AM I DRIVING?* signs.

Yeah, she knew. It had been announced to the department. I wondered if she was aware she would be the one to field any calls resulting from the signs. Yeah, she knew that, too.

I told her the company had agreed to pay her $3 for each call she received. Yup, she knew that, too. She said Blake Richardson told her about it. He made it sound like he was doing that voluntarily . . . out of the goodness of his heart.

Blaze said she wasn't concerned about the additional workload in any event. She said she doubted anyone would make calls to business establishments as a result of those kinds of signs.

"Are you coming to the union meeting tomorrow night?" I asked, knowing she'd be there. She was a good-union gal. She was always at the meetings.

"Of course I'll be there," she assured me, "I'm always there."

"Don't let anything you hear at the meeting upset you," I advised. "Just remember, whatever happens, you'll be receiving three dollars a call."

"Why? What's going to happen?"

"You'll hear at the meeting."

That pretty much concluded the business part of our evening. After three or four more drinks, I decided to test the water. I suggested that she and I might meet again socially without the need of a business discussion.

Blaze cocked her head and smiled. A very enchanting smile. She said my suggestion would be very nice, but she doubted her boyfriend would agree. Shit, I didn't know she had a boyfriend.

Before Blaze and I kissed goodnight – don't get excited, it was just a quick peck and a friendly embrace – I asked her to provide me with a list of district managers, their truck numbers and the locations of their routes.

The union meeting the next night was held at the *PAR 5 COUNTRY CLUB* - West Bridgewater/Brockton line. It was owned by my good friend, Henry Nickalou. Henry let us use the place for nothing.

As you've no doubt guessed because of its name, the *Par 5* was a golf club and a lounge that golfers could retreat to and relax, drink and socialize after their 18 holes. There was a large function room behind the lounge, ideal for parties and dances . . . or a union meeting.

Henry let us use the place for nothing. Obviously, aside from being a good guy and a friend of mine and the working class, Henry did a hefty business at the bar any night we had a meeting. Newspaper folk, after all, in addition to being constant seekers of truth, justice and the American way, are also drinkers.

Those who arrived early drank before the meeting and virtually everybody who attended drank – heartily – after the meeting. I was forced to make a ruling, however, that there would be no liquor in the meeting, itself. That edict was made after a particularly heated meeting resulted in beer bottles being tossed across the room in fits of anger. Nobody, fortunately, was struck, but several members were sprayed by the beer that made Milwaukee famous.

At the current meeting, I asked the lovely Blaze Starr to hand out lists of district managers, their truck numbers and the locations of their routes and, on each slip of paper, the telephone number the public was urged to report *HOW AM I DRIVING?*

I told our union members: "Pass the telephone number out to your wives, husbands, other members of your family and friends. Have them call that number, report the truck number and location and note the perfectly wonderful way the vehicle was being operated. When your friend or relative has completed the call, have them hang up and immediately call again with a separate report. If the line is busy, have then call again and again and again until he or she gets through. And then repeat the procedure . . . again and again. If you have a day off Monday through Friday, do it yourselves. Call and call again. We want a deluge of calls reporting how wonderfully our district managers are operating their vehicles. Pass it around! Stress it! Make this work!"

Bingo!

After editing stories and *laying out* the pages I was assigned the following Monday, I contacted *The Examiner* telephone operator and asked for an outside line. I punched in the number that appeared on the rear of the trucks.

Busy . . . busy . . . busy.

Beautiful.

Finally: *"Examiner* circulation hotline."

"Hello there."

Blaze apparently knew my voice right away.

"Rocky. . ." she began.

"No, my name is Fred," I interrupted. "Um. . . Fred Flintstone. I just called to tell you I observed Truck Number 14 being driven in East Bridgewater and the operator handled it beautifully. He obeyed the speed limit, stayed within the lines and was extremely considerate to pedestrians."

"Thank you for calling and telling us that, sir. We appreciate it," Blaze dutifully responded.

As soon as I hung up, I went through *The Examiner* operator again, asking for an outside line again and it was busy again.

Finally, after three and a half minutes of busy signals: *Examiner* circulation hotline."

"Hello."

"Rocky."

"No, this is Dwight Eisenhower. I was just driving behind Truck Number 7 in Abington and the operator was the finest I've ever witnessed. I told my wife, Mamie, I simply must call the number posted and praise his driving."

"Thanks so much for calling and telling us that, sir, we appreciate it."

Two minutes later – after several more attempts – *"Examiner* circulation hotline."

"Well, hello there."

"Rocky, I know it's you. I know your voice."

"Well, OK, Blaze, I appreciate the fact that you know my voice and I love you, too. For your report, you received a call reporting the sighting of Truck 21 in North Easton; great driving."

"Thanks so much for calling and telling us that. We really appreciate it and, Rocky, I'm so busy answering telephone calls that I don't have time to do my regular work."

"Don't worry about it. It's Richardson's problem. At three dollars a call; you're gonna be rich!"

Fairly early the next morning, crusty, old managing editor Hugh Beckerman shouted: "Scarpati!"

When I looked up from my layout of Page Two, Beckerman spat: "William Casey wants to see you!"

And when I didn't move quickly enough: "NOW!"

Examiner Publisher William J. Casey III didn't get up to his feet and walk around his massive desk to shake my hand the way he generally did. I wondered previously if he did that for everybody who walked into his office or if that particular graciousness was reserved for the union president. It didn't matter. It didn't happen this time.

He looked up from a paper he appeared to be studying and, barely moving his lips, spouted: "What do you hear? What do you say?" That was William's standard greeting. It was from an old Cagney movie. William bore a startling resemblance to Cagney. I once pointed out to him that the "What-do-you-hear? What-do-you-say?" line was from an old Cagney movie. He said he was very much aware of that and asked if it was from *WHITE HEAT* . . . I told him, "No, it was from *ANGELS WITH DIRTY FACES*."

"We have a young lady who works downstairs in the Circulation Department; her name is Blaze Starr," William began.

"Yes, I know her. Everybody within a 50-mile radius of Brockton knows her," I responded.

"Yes, I'm well aware that you know her," Casey spat. "Blaze Starr, what kind of name is that anyway? What is she, a former stripper?"

"That I wouldn't know."

"In any event, yesterday she answered the telephone 331 times. . ."

"Ah-ha."

". . . And earned 993 dollars."

I didn't say anything at that point.

"Her earnings were the result of a deal you made with Blake Richardson to allow him to place certain signs on the backs of trucks."

"I don't think it had anything to do with *allowing* him to put the signs on the trucks. He was going to do that anyway. The payment was to compensate Ms. Starr for her increased workload."

"In any event, Ms. Starr is to receive three dollars per call for her *increased work load,*" Casey spat.

"Yup, that's correct."

"Well, I've been notified that at a union meeting you told all the members of your union to have their friends and family call the posted number and report that every district manager's driving was hunky dory. Don't lie to me now, Richardson's buddy, Bill, was at the meeting and reported what happened."

"I wouldn't lie to you, William, I'm guilty as charged. That's exactly what happened. And I'd have told you that even without Bill's testimony."

"Blake Richardson told me what you did is grounds for dismissal and he wants me to fire you."

"It's not grounds for dismissal, but you wouldn't fire me in any event."

"Why not?"

"Because I'm good at my job on the desk and you respect what I do as union president. You enjoy sparring with me on union issues."

"But the payments to Ms. Starr have to cease," Williams noted, still barely moving his lips. I'm telling you, the dude should have been a ventriloquist. "They have to cease today. I can't afford to pay some stripper 993 dollars a day to answer phones."

"Hey, that's not fair, we don't know that's she's a stripper or ever was a stripper for that matter. She might have been a porn star."

"The payments have to stop," Casey insisted.

"If the payments have to end today; then the signs have to end today."

"They're coming off the trucks as we speak."

"While I've got your attention, I'd like to talk to you about one other issue," I said.

I told William about the problem I had with the re-assignment of Jose Cervantes from the shipping room to the road.

Casey shook his head.

"I can't do a thing for you about that," he insisted.

That afternoon, all *Examiner* trucks left the newspaper building with four holes in the rear where bolts had once held signs inquiring: *HOW AM I DRIVING?*

CHAPTER 22

TORN BETWEEN TWO LOVERS?

I walked out of *The Examiner* that day and was immediately confronted by Barbara's big, old, blue car – the size of a boat – sitting in the no-parking zone. Barbara behind the wheel.

I took a deep breath – exhaled – and opened the passenger door and slid inside. She was wearing the skin-tight jeans she was always so very fond of and a tight jersey, her nipples bulging. Braless, of course. She had very firm breasts – not huge; sexy.

"I heard you were with a very sexy blonde at the *Palace Hotel* last week," Barbara noted without bothering to say hello.

"How the hell did you hear that?" I responded.

Once again, if they ever made a movie about our love affair – Barbara's and mine – this is where they'd have to have music in the background.

Every breath you take
Every move you make
Every bond you break
Every step you take
I'll be watching you.

"Did you take her upstairs and screw her?"

"No."

"You wouldn't tell me if you did."

"Sure, I would; what reason would I have to lie about that now? Besides, you were always the one to cheat and lie about it after."

Barbara didn't respond to that.

"Like the *old friend* you *scored pot for* the last night we were together."

Barbara remained silent.

Finally: "You know I still love you."

"I still love you," I responded and questioned myself if I were lying. I knew I missed the hell out of her.

"Let's get back together," she suggested.

"That's a bad idea," I said.

"Why?"

"Because I'd end up killing you. That's how domestic violence works. It escalates."

"It doesn't have to."

I got out of the car and watched her drive away.

It would have been so easy to agree and get back together. That summer on Green Street was the most depressing time of my life. I went to work. I left work and drank. Went to my room and slept. No money. It went to child support and booze. And a very little bit of it went to pay the rent. I purchased a tiny black-and-white portable TV for my room. Didn't matter. I didn't watch it. And Labor Day came and went. Another holiday without Barbara.

Early in September I received a voice message from Eva at work. My heart pounded when I recognized her voice. She didn't need to identify herself.

"It's me," she had said. "I wanted to talk."

I wished I had been at my desk to receive the call.

She hadn't left a number where I could reach her. That was consistent with what she had said all along. There couldn't be any connection between us. Not until after *the Incredible Hulk's* murder trial. I assumed she was calling me from a payphone.

I received the exact same message on my voice mail at work a couple of days later and cursed myself again for not being at my desk when she called.

Saturday night, September 11, 1976, I was sitting at the bar in *The Palace Hotel.*

Making love to my tonic and gin?

Nope, I was still drinking vodka and tonic.

The pay phone rang and rang and rang in the hallway leading to and from the lounge.

I paid it no mind.

Finally, "Rocky Scarpati!" someone shouted from the hallway. "Telephone!"

I got to my feet and made my way to the telephone, a bit of a stagger in my step.

Whoever had taken the call left the receiver hanging against the wall.

"Hello."

"Hi."

My heart stopped a moment.

"How have you been?" Eva asked.

"Missing you. Missing the hell out of you."

"I miss you too. But our time is coming. Everything is coming to an end. We can be together soon. Maurice's trial has been set for Monday, September 20. We can be together after the trial. Are you and Barbara still split?"

"Yeah, she wants to get back together, though. But we're still split."

"Oh," Eva sounded somewhat deflated. "You're seeing her then. Talking to her."

"She was parked in front of *The Examiner* one day when I left work. We talked, that's all. She wanted to get back together. I told her, 'No way.'"

"I love you, Rocky."

I had no way of knowing if that was true.

143

But I'd take it.
"I love you, too."
I really had no idea if we were in love.
I figured we must have been at least in lust.
Such a beautiful woman.

CHAPTER 23

JUST SOME GUY . . .

This time when I entered his office, I beat William to the punch: "What do you hear? What do you say?"

A slight smile from Casey and then: "You dirty rat!"

"Despite impressionists' insistence on using the line, Cagney never said that in a movie" I commented.

"I know it," Williams agreed, "he should have."

At that point, he got up from his desk, took the long walk around it and shook my hand.

After he returned to his spot behind the wooden monstrosity, he sat back down, lit a cigarette.

I said: "The trial of Maurice diMontiferro begins September 20th in Providence Superior Court, Are we going to cover it?"

"Why would we; is there a local angle?"

"Sure, diMontiferro stands accused of killing none other than Angelo Macrillo, the dude who was arrested for the murder of Lou Montgomery. And the one and only Lou Montgomery, you'll recall, is the gentleman I was accused of beating to death in a Providence parking garage."

"Well then. . ." William Casey leaned back in his plush, high-backed, leather desk chair and appeared to give the matter careful consideration before speaking: ". . . why would you want us covering this Maurice character's trial? It seems to me, any story we run about his trial would have to include the fact that you went to trial on a murder charge."

I responded: "Just like the late-great P.T. Barnum once said: 'I don't care what you say about me. Just spell my name right.'"

Casey took a long drag, leaned back and said: "You don't really mean that, Rocky."

"No, I don't. But most people believe, just because you're found not guilty of a crime, it doesn't mean that you didn't do it. A lot of people believe I offed Montgomery."

"Offed?"

"Yeah, offed. Knocked off; tough-guy talk for killed.

"Anyhow, there are a lot of people who are convinced that I'm, in fact, a murderer. I know by the way they look at me in the street or around the city. But then Angel – that's Angelo Macrillo – was charged with the same murder and I figured a lot of people who had convicted me in their hearts and minds might have had second thoughts."

Casey picked up on my reference to Macrillo.

"Angel, huh," he repeated, "What's that all about; do you know him intimately?"

William's response shook me a little bit.

"No, I just heard from my sources that Macrillo goes by the nickname, *Angel*."

I wondered if Casey detected a lack of conviction in my voice.

"Anyhow, people might now think, 'Yeah, this Angel character probably did it. It wasn't Scarpati after all.'

"You know, if Macrillo had ever gone to trial and been convicted, that would have clinched it. But now that will never happen. And I don't want people to forget another man was arrested for the crime I was charged with. Hey, maybe something will come out at Maurice What's-His-Name's trial that will prove Angel actually was the murderer. I'd like to know what happens at his trial in Providence."

"I just don't really get it, Rocky. I don't get your keen interest about something happening in Providence to people you don't know.

146

You *don't know* this Angel character, do you; you didn't kill him, did you?" William chuckled.

"Don't be ridiculous!"

After I caught my breath, Casey threw up the metaphoric white flag and said: "OK, OK, you convinced me. I don't know why, but we'll cover the damn trial. But it won't be you covering it! Somehow, I get the impression that would be a definite conflict of interest."

"Never in my wildest dreams did I ever expect I'd be assigned to it, William."

Although, you know and I know, folks, there's nothing I'd like better than to be a fly on the wall and hear what's taking place in connection with the state of Rhode Island vs. Maurice diMontiferro.

"I'll tell Hugh Beckerman to take Audacity off the district court beat for a couple of weeks and have her cover the trial in Providence. You can cover the district court for her."

My heart skipped a beat two nights later when Audacity – looking as outlandish yet outlandishly charming as hell – reached across the linen clothed table and placed her hand on mine. We were at *Capeway*– the restaurant, not the nightclub attached to it– drinking and feasting on *Capeway's* specialty, prime rib. Audacity was drinking wine. Per usual, I had a vodka and tonic.

"So tell me again, Audacity, why I'm taking you out tonight."

"Well, as you're aware, I've been assigned to the Maurice diMonterro murder case in Providence. His victim, Angelo . . . um, Angelo whatever his name is . . ."

"Macrillo," I provided the surname for her.

"Yes, his victim, Angelo Macrillo, had been accused of killing the same man you once went to trial for killing."

"That's right."

"Hugh Beckerman told me that's a tidbit that should be mentioned in all my stories about the trial."

"OK."

"Well, I thought maybe you should tell me about it."

147

"That's all there is to tell. I was accused of killing the same man Macrillo was accused of killing."

"That's all?" she asked, sounding deflated.

"That's all."

"Then I guess I asked you to take me out under false pretenses," Audacity said. "I thought there'd be more."

"Could I have your telephone number?" I asked.

She recited her telephone extension at work.

"No, I mean your home number," I said.

"Why? Do you want to ask me out on a date?"

"Well . . . well . . . sure, I'd love to ask you for a date, but the reason I was asking . . . I'm hoping you'll give me reports about what's happening at the trial. You know, more detail than what will be in the paper . . . in your stories. That's why I asked for your number."

"If that's the real reason you want my number, then no, you can't have it. I work – and report to – Hugh Beckerman, not to you."

"But, if I told you I wanted your number to ask you out on a date, you'd give it to me?"

"Yeah, if you were going to ask me for a date."

"Well, yeah, I'd love to take you out."

"Now I don't know whether to believe you," Audacity protested. "I'll give you my number *after* the trial."

"And then you'll go out with me?"

"I didn't say that," she responded. "I'll let you know after the trial."

"Can I ask you a personal question?"

"I could say, 'No,' but somehow I expect that you'd ask anyway," she said.

"I mean absolutely no offense by this, but I'm wondering, why *do you* wear so *much* makeup."

"How am I *not supposed* to be offended by that?"

"You're such a natural beauty, why bother with so much makeup and heavy lipstick. It looks kind of . . . kind of . . . well, kind of clownish."

"My parents were clowns . . . both of them. Maybe that has something to do with it. Maybe it's in my blood. . . If you think I look so funny, why are you so interested in me?"

"Because you're very beautiful and charming and as my friend Tony Lombardi used to say, 'You've got a body like a brick shithouse and not a brick's outta place.'"

"If I had a dime for every time I heard that."

"You'd be a rich woman, huh?"

"No, I'd have ten cents. You've got no couth, Rocky!"

After dinner was served and Audacity was cutting into her prime rib – she ordered it *well done,* she killed it – she confessed: "You know that first day in the office when you recognized me from *Capeway* and I said I didn't remember?"

"Yeah, it broke my heart. I kind of imagined we were really getting into each other that night."

"We were. I remembered you from that night. I remembered you very well."

"Then why did you say you didn't remember me?"

"I didn't want you to be too sure of yourself."

"Well, how about the next time, the time I saw you leaving with that guy, the ugly one?"

"Yeah, I remember that night, too. He wasn't ugly."

"Who was that guy?"

"He was just some guy I left with."

CHAPTER 24

THE SMOKING GUN

We appeared to be getting along so famously that I obviously didn't want the night to end. I was so certain she was flirting with me. You heard the conversation. Wasn't she flirting? So I suggested we leave the restaurant and go into the lounge for a few more drinks and dancing.

Audacity declined.

Said she had plans for the evening.

Obviously, I wondered about those plans; but I didn't ask. I didn't want to appear insecure.

I remained in the office late on Monday, September 20th, the first day of the diMontiferro trial. I told myself it was to write that week's column for the editorial page, but it was more likely because I was waiting for Audacity to return from court. I had no idea how much Audacity would have to report – either to me or her reading public – as a result of the first day. It was possible that they might not even have a jury selected.

But I was shocked when Audacity stepped off the elevator and into the newsroom much earlier than I would have expected. I worried a little bit that the trial may have been postponed. I mean, I had waited for what seemed like an eternity for *The Incredible Hulk's* day in court. I just wanted the drama to end. But the other thing that really shocked me when Audacity stepped off the elevator was that she wasn't wearing a ton of eye makeup. And her lipstick – always that overbearing red – was a very pale pink and was spread sparingly.

"Why are you back so soon, Audacity?"

I was expecting the worst.

"Jury selection was pretty much a breeze," she responded, "then the judge called for opening arguments and then called it a day."

"Opening statements," I said.

"What?"

"When attorneys talk to the jury at the end of a trial, that's closing *arguments*. At the start of a case, that's opening *statements*."

"I thank you for that," Audacity responded.

I couldn't tell if she was being sarcastic because I had corrected her.

"So tell me about opening statements."

"I'm not going to do that now," she said. "I've got a story to write. I don't want to be here all night. Take me to dinner when I'm done. I'll tell you about opening argu . . . opening statements then."

Music to my ears. Sure, I was anxious to hear about what went on in court, but I also figured Audacity was implying she wanted to spend more time with me.

"Another dinner, huh," I responded. "If this trial lasts very long, I'll have to file for bankruptcy."

"I'll let you off easy tonight," she said. "Ever been to the *Sherwood Café* in Randolph? They have the best pizza around."

Another chorus of music to my ears. I knew that Audacity had an apartment in Randolph, a hop, skip and jump from Brockton. Obviously, what she had in mind was a few slices of pizza, some drinks and then back to her place for a nightcap."

"Pizza sounds great."

I've got to interrupt myself right here to tell you about pizza in New England. It's the best pizza in the world. Not just any pizza in New England, but the pies that are known as *bar pizza*.

Saying that is one of the greatest conversation starters in the world. Everybody and his brother has an opinion about pizza. I'm certain that people from Chicago with their famed *deep-dish pizza* would gasp if you told them slices in New England were far and away better. Listen to a dude from the Big Apple and he's going to insist *New York-style* pizza can't be beaten. But they're all wrong. New England has the greatest bar pizza. I'm sure there are people in Italy who would call me crazy. But I've never been to Italy. So I'll just say I sincerely doubt the pizza there could be any better than New England *bar pizza.*

"Have you ever had baked-bean pizza?" Audacity asked.

Whoa, New England *bar* pizza is one thing, but let's not get carried away here!

I guess Audacity could conclude from the expression on my face that I had never had the *pleasure.* To be perfectly clear, I had never given a thought that anyone would ever consider making a baked-bean pizza. Never mind bite into one.

"You've got to try it," Audacity insisted. "It's what the *Sherwood Café* is known for, a baked-bean special made with baked beans, salami and onion."

"I don't know, Audacity. I just don't know."

"You've got to try it!"

Audacity led the way in her car, I followed in mine; we took the main drag out of The Shoe City; did I ever mention that Brockton was once famous for shoes; known as the *Shoe Capitol of the World*? Anyhow, we took the main drag out of Brockton, through the tiny town of Avon and into Randolph; a right at a large automobile dealership, through a heavy wooded area and there it was, the *Sherwood Café.* Observing all the trees in the immediate proximity, I noted that "it should have been called *Sherwood Forest.*"

"How about if we order two pizzas, one baked-bean special and the other pepperoni?" I suggested. "Then we can each have some of both."

"I don't like pepperoni!" Audacity said with certainty.

"Well, what other kind do you like?"

"Mushroom."

"OK, then we'll order a baked-bean special and a mushroom."

153

She agreed.

While we waited for our order to be filled, I gazed into Audacity's scarcely made up eyes. I reached across the table and took her hand. I hadn't even done it consciously. It just happened.

"You know, I think I made a mistake," I confessed. "As wholesomely and absolutely beautiful as you look right now, I don't think I should have advised you to change your eye makeup. With that, you were uniquely striking, stunning. Right now, although you still may have the most brilliant eyes I've seen, you're still just another beautiful woman. When you cut back on the makeup, I think you lost your identity."

"And what about the lipstick?" she asked.

"As delightful and comfortable and gentle as the pale pink is, it's not you. Go back to the brilliant red. Besides, you've got your parents' reputation to live up to."

"My parents' reputation?"

"Yeah, as clowns."

We chatted for a while longer and then Audacity asked: "So, do you want to hear about opening statements?"

"Yeah, it's the reason we're here, isn't it? Or are we just here to get to know one another better?"

"Nope, we're here to talk about the trial. The opening statements today were dynamic."

That sent shivers up my spine. Obviously, I wanted the prosecution's opening to be dynamic. Not so much from the defense. I simply needed a conviction. For my peace of mind. I needed *The Hulk* to be convicted and Angel's murder to be put to bed. So, if anyone was going to be dynamic, I wanted it to be the prosecutor.

"Who's the prosecutor in the case?" I asked.

"A young man by the name of Peter Constable. Very young, I thought, to be trying a murder case. About our age. Tall, dark and extremely handsome."

"Just like the dude I saw you leaving *Capeway* with that night?"

154

"Don't be silly, he wasn't handsome. Intriguing maybe. Certainly not handsome. . . Do you want to hear about opening statements or not?"

I just nodded at that point.

"This Peter Constable is a showman. It was almost as if he was an actor playing a part. He stood in front of the jury box, then paced. Stopped, paced back to the center of the jury box and stopped again. He brushed his brilliantly dark black hair from his eyes and said something to the effect of: '"You know, I'm a fairly new assistant district attorney. This is my first murder case. When I was told I was being assigned a murder case, I became very nervous. But, when I was handed this case, the State of Rhode Island v. Maurice diMonteferro, and read the file, I breathed a sigh of relief.'

"Then he said something like there was no way he was going to lose this one and the defense attorney leaped to his feet, apparently to object, but even before he could, the judge warned, 'Watch yourself, Mr. Constable.'

"Then, undeterred, Constable picked up his narrative: 'The police in Pawtucket received a telephone call at precisely 10:33 p.m. on Tuesday, November 25, of last year from an unidentified female, who reported that she was driving past 1025 Seacrest Avenue, Pawtucket, a rural, backwoods road, only minutes before, when she heard what appeared to be gunshots. Police dispatched to the Seacrest Avenue address reported that they arrived on the scene at approximately 10:45. The responding officers entered the small bungalow to find the defendant, Maurice diMoniferro standing over the victim, Angelo Macrillo, with a smoking gun in his hand.'"

"'Objection, Your Honor,' the defense attorney bellowed even before he got to his feet."

"The judge called the attorneys to her bench for a conference."

"It's called a sidebar conference," I informed Audacity.

"Yeah, right, well after the conference, the judge told jurors whatever lawyers say in their openings is not evidence and only what they hear testified to under oath is evidence. She told them to disregard anything Constable said about *a smoking gun*. She said she believed even the district attorney would agree the gun wasn't literally smoking."

"'Yes, I agree the gun in the hand of the defendant, Maurice diMontiferro, wasn't literally smoking,'" Constable said.

"Constable told jurors it wasn't necessary for the government to prove a motive in the case, but Maurice diMontiferro had the oldest motive in the world. 'He was on the short end of a love triangle.' Constable said. It seems that Angelo Macrillo's fiancé, a woman by the name of Eva Green, was diMonteferro's girlfriend before she met Macrillo."

That little bit of baffling information drove me much more than a little bit crazy, but I tried not to show it.

"Constable said: 'To be perfectly honest, as I indicated before, I wasn't all too confident and happy about trying a murder case so early in my career. I guess I can only be thankful and grateful to District Attorney Anthony Fazio for assigning me to one in which the defendant was apprehended holding a smok . . . a murder weapon."

"So how about the defense attorney, was the defense attorney as dynamic as the prosecutor?"

Much to my dismay, Audacity replied: "Even more dynamic!"

"More dynamic?"

"Yeah, for sure. He told jurors he was not only going to convince them that his client was not guilty beyond a reasonable doubt, but he was also going to tell them who actually did the shooting."

I felt like I had been punched in the stomach.

The vodka and tonic I was drinking went down the wrong way. I coughed violently.

"Who is the defense attorney, anyway?" I asked.

"Richard Egbert."

I gulped. Nearly began another coughing spell. This conversation could be the death of me. You may recall, Richie Egbert is the attorney I arranged to represent Gregory Davies in his suit against the Randolph police. Gregory Davies, the dude who was shot and crippled by the cops when he exited his car on Route 24. Gregory Davies, the dude I was with and introduced to Barbara the night I beat the shit out of her. So Richie Egbert was defending Maurice diMonteferro and Richie Egbert just happened to be the best defense attorney in the great Commonwealth of Massachusetts. Well, Egbert was the best defense attorney in the Bay State with the possible exception of Kevin Reddington. And maybe F. Lee Bailey.

"Richie Egbert, if it's the same Richie Egbert I'm thinking of, is an attorney in Massachusetts. How the hell is he defending a murder client in Rhode Island?" I asked, kind of hoping he wasn't. I mean, Richie Egbert was that good. I didn't want him near the Maurice diMonteferro case.

"I don't know," Audacity responded. "I'll ask him."

"Maybe he's not the same Richie Egbert," I noted, kind of silently praying that might be true.

"This Richie Egbert is a little guy," Audacity said. "Curly hair and a very brash, husky voice."

"Yup, that's Richie alright," I conceded. "Ask him what he's doing defending a murderer in Rhode Island."

"Defending a murderer?" Audacity asked. "Don't you mean defending a murder suspect? I mean, isn't he innocent until proven guilty?"

"Yup, as innocent and pure as the freshly fallen snow. And with a guy like Egbert defending him, he may remain that way."

Two bites into the baked-bean special I was convinced we should have ordered two of them and to hell with the mushroom. It was the best pizza I had ever tasted.

"I know Richie Egbert, he's good; he's very good," I said now to Audacity.

"He certainly is if he can follow through on his promise to tell jurors who actually did the shooting."

"He said that?" I couldn't believe it. "He actually said he was going to reveal the murderer?"

"Well, I may be paraphrasing a little bit," Audacity allowed. She referred to her notebook.

"He said, 'By the end of the trial, you will not only have a reasonable doubt that my client murdered the victim, but you will have a very good idea who actually pulled the trigger.'

"Do you realize you just turned white?" Audacity asked. "You don't have a vested interest in this trial, do you?"

"No, of course not; not beyond the one you already know about.

"Richie Egbert never ceases to amaze me," I noted. "When you talked to Richie after the proceeding, did you ask him who he was referring to? Did you ask him who he's going to reveal?"

"No, I'm certain he wouldn't tell me that at this point, anyway."

"No, I'm sure he wouldn't," I had to agree, "but I think I would have asked.

"What else did he have to say?"

"Not much; his opening was very short and sweet. Just the usual shit. He told jurors to keep an open mind while the prosecution was presenting its case. But then, out of nowhere, he dropped the bomb. Out of nowhere he said he was going to let jurors know who did it."

I'm telling you; it was almost enough for me to lose my appetite.

It's just that that baked-bean special was so goddamn good!

"Oh, by the way," Audacity said, "My parents weren't really clowns. My father was an accountant and my mother was a real estate agent."

"Why did you say they were clowns?"

"I wanted to make you feel bad for talking about my heavy eye makeup and lipstick; calling me clownish!"

"I didn't call you clownish."

"You made me feel very bad."

"Well, if it makes you feel any better, you look great tonight. Very striking with the heavy makeup. You look like you and you're very beautiful."

CHAPTER 25

SOME CHICKS DON'T GET GOT!

"Well, what did you think? Was the baked-bean pizza as good as I said it was or not?" Audacity asked as I was walking her to her car after dinner."

"Yes, I certainly have to admit. It was the best pizza I've had anytime. Anywhere."

When we reached her car, I took her into my arms and gave her the deepest, most abiding kiss anyone has ever delivered since Beethoven penned *The Moonlight Sonata*. Shit, to be perfectly honest, I don't even recall if there *was* a moon that night. Our tongues danced together and I think I was more excited than I ever had been since some well-intentioned doctor slapped me at birth.

"So are you going to invite me back to your apartment for a nightcap?" I asked feeling about as confident as a high-stakes Vegas gambler with a pair of loaded dice in the palm of his hand and declaring, "Baby needs a new pair of shoes!"

"No, I'm not," Audacity responded firmly.

"No? Why not?" I asked, my confidence suddenly shattered.

I never could figure Audacity out. I mean, I knew we had a tremendous connection. I felt the attraction that very first night when we kept stealing glances – hell, more than glances; we were drowning in one another's eyes. Yup, I felt the attraction that first night at *Capeway*. I felt it again when I saw her leaving *Capeway* with the as yet to be identified dude. So now I ask her if she's planning to invite me back to her place for a nightcap and she says, "No." I felt like telling her that her outward display of confidence – if that's, indeed, what it was – was not attractive. What I did say was: "You know, some chicks who play hard to get don't get got!" Then I asked again: "Why not, why aren't you inviting me back?"

"Well, for one thing, I'm fresh out of vodka," Audacity said.

"No problem," I responded. "We'll stop at a packie."

"It's late," Audacity said. "I think I better get home and get to bed."

Which, of course, was pretty much what I had in mind in any event, but I didn't specify it.

"After the trial, I'll give you my home telephone number and you can use it to ask me out on a real date, then I'll invite you back to my place for a nightcap."

I accepted that begrudgingly. But, hell, I didn't even know if I'd be longing to date Audacity after the trial. I was expecting to rekindle the fire with Eva Green post trial. But I said, "Yeah, OK, I'll ask you for a date after the trial." And then I told Audacity to ask Richie Egbert whatever happened regarding the Gregory Davies' case. She asked who Gregory Davies was and I explained how I had set him up with Richie Egbert to sue the pants off the Town of Randolph for the outrageous way the cops shot and crippled him.

The next day after court, Audacity . . . well, she looked absolutely stunning when she stepped off the elevator. Her dress, a brilliant red that matched her flaming lipstick, revealed an abundance of cleavage on the top and plenty of leg beneath. It certainly would have been ultimately more appropriate for a nightclub as opposed to courtroom attire. She must have turned heads and been met with more than one gasp earlier in the day, I imagined.

"I can't go to dinner with you tonight," she volunteered straight out of the starting gate when I left my desk to greet her the moment she stepped out of the elevator.

"Oh yeah, heavy date?" I responded, my heart breaking. "Maybe with that young and extremely handsome assistant district attorney you find so incredibly desirable?"

"No, nothing as exciting as that. My uncle is in town on business – well, he's in Boston from New York – and he's taking me to dinner. When I write my story, I'll have to run right along, but I'll print out a copy so you'll know what happened today."

"If you dress that way for your uncle, I'd hate to imagine what you would look like on an actual date."

"I don't think it would be that hard for you to imagine. I mean, keeping in mind the cock teaser that I am."

"Cock teaser?"

"Yeah, isn't that exactly what you had in mind when you were telling me that 'some chicks who play hard to get don't get got'?"

"Oh, come on, Audacity; I didn't mean it as an insult."

"I don't know how it could be taken any other way," she insisted.

"In any event, call me after the trial and we'll see how much of a tease I can – or won't – be."

Wow!

Intriguing offer. One that would be very difficult to refuse. Especially when she was standing right there in front of me looking beautiful as all hell.

"So now let me get busy on my story or I'll be terribly late and you'll have to answer to my uncle."

Audacity turned toward her desk, but then hesitated and turned back.

"Oh, by the way, I asked Attorney Egbert about that guy – the one that was shot in the leg and crippled. I asked Egbert how the case was going. He said it wasn't going anywhere. He said your friend flunked the polygraph."

I couldn't goddamn believe it! I couldn't believe that Richie wasn't taking the case just because Gregory Davies flunked the polygraph. I mean, everybody knows that polygraph tests aren't reliable. That's why their results aren't admissible in court – they're unreliable.

That got me to wondering, though. Everybody knows that some dudes can beat the polygraph. Some dudes can tell bald-face lies and the machine reports they're being truthful. But now I wondered if someone can tell the truth and the machine register that he's lying?

It would be hard to imagine that it wasn't what happened in this case. I mean, if the cops' version of events was the truth, that would mean that Gregory Davies was passing by them on the highway and he opened fire on them for absolutely no reason at all. What dude in his right mind would ever take pot shots at the cops for absolutely no reason at all? And certainly Gregory Davies appeared to be in his right mind. And, besides that, the cops never came up with a gun that could conceivably be put in Gregory Davies' hand. God only knows how in hell the gun that was found (directly behind a rock) could have been tossed from a passing motor vehicle.

I felt bad. I felt really bad. I felt terrible that Richie Egbert wasn't taking the case simply because Gregory Davies flunked a polygraph. I didn't give a shit what the polygraph said. I still believed Davies. Too bad I never got Gregory's telephone number so I could tell him I still believed him. I would have set him up with another attorney to represent him.

Moments later, Audacity was working feverishly on her story regarding *The Commonwealth v Maurice diMontiferro*. When she was finished, she printed it out as promised, waltzed by my desk with the cutest little sway of her hips and ass and flipped the story onto it without saying a word.

It went like this:

PROVIDENCE, R.I. -The Pawtucket patrolman, who arrested Maurice diMontiferro on a charge of first-degree murder in the Nov. 25, 1975, shooting death of a reputed Providence drug kingpin and hit man, said he nabbed the defendant as he stood over the victim's body with the proverbial smoking gun in his hand.

diMontiferro, 42, of 1503 Anderson Drive, Providence, is accused of pumping two bullets into the back of Angelo "Angel" Macrillo, in a small bungalow in a heavily wooded area of Pawtucket. The dramatic assertion by the arresting patrolman came in the first day of testimony of diMontiferro's trial in the Superior Courthouse.

It was the second time jurors had been told the tall, brawny defendant was apprehended with a "smoking gun." In making his opening statement to jurors the previous day, Assistant District Attorney Peter Constable told them that's exactly what they would hear. At the time, though, the "smoking-gun" disclosure raised an objection from Defense Attorney Richard Egbert and that objection was sustained.

Obviously when the characterization was repeated in the patrolman's testimony, it sparked the same objection by Attorney Egbert that resulted in the same ruling from Judge Carlotta Abernathy.

Seemingly undaunted by the ruling, Constable asked: "The gun you observed the defendant holding when you arrested him wasn't literally smoking, was it?"

"No, it wasn't," Patrolman Ronald Rollins responded.

"Then why did you describe it as a smoking gun?" Constable asked.

"Because, when the defendant dropped it as ordered, I immediately picked it up and smelled the barrel. It had recently been fired. It might as well have been smoking."

Egbert was on his feet again. "Your honor."

"Yes, jurors will disregard the comment, 'It might as well have been smoking.'" And, then turning to the witness she said, "Please just respond to the questions without adding your opinion, patrolman."

"Yes, Your Honor."

Constable asked if the gun was tested for fingerprints.

"Yes, it was."

"And what did the test reveal?"

"Just the defendant, Maurice diMontiferro's, fingerprints."

"Nobody else's prints on the gun?"

"No, nobody else's."

"And when bullets were removed from the victim's body were they tested to determine if they came from the weapon the defendant was holding?"

"Yes, they were tested."

"And what did that ballistics test reveal?"

"The weapon the defendant was holding was the murder weapon."

"Another reason for labeling it as the smoking gun?" Constable suggested, but immediately said he'd withdraw that statement.

The victim in the case, Angelo "Angel" Macrillo, who police noted has been a suspect in more than one previous homicide, had recently been arrested and charged with beating and killing a PROVIDENCE CHRONICLE employee in a downtown parking garage in that city. The victim in that case, Lou Montgomery, a union leader at the Providence paper, was the same man Enterprise columnist Rocco Scarpati was previously charged with slaying. Scarpati was tried and found not guilty of that charge.

What you have to remember at this point is that Audacity was writing this article on Tuesday night to appear in Wednesday afternoon's newspaper. She wrote:

The prosecution was expected to rest its case at some point today. Maurice diMontiferro is expected to testify in his own defense.

CHAPTER 26
THE LONE RANGER RIDES AGAIN

Did you ever question The Lone Ranger's judgment? For those of you too young to remember, The Lone Ranger was a masked man who rode his trusty steed, Silver, around the Wild West with his faithful native-American companion, Tonto. They made a habit of rescuing beautiful young maidens in distress and, instead of hanging around to be properly rewarded, the Lone Ranger would merely hand them a silver bullet and ride off into the sunset.

After reading Audacity's story detailing Tuesday's courtroom events, I needed a drink. But I didn't need to be drinking and laughing and chatting with a group of people I knew. The usual watering holes were out of bounds. I needed a place where I could sit. Think. Meditate. I picked a joint on Montello Street. Sort of a dive. I had tipped a few drinks there once before. Many months ago. I actually had picked up a chick there. But that wasn't my intention this particular night.

I walked in and sat at the bar. There were only a few people in the joint, 10 or12 folks sitting at tables. I couldn't help but notice this one particular girl seated at the bar. Pretty much the other end of the bar, actually. She was attractive as hell. Long, straight brown hair and slender. She didn't look like she belonged there. Too reserved. Sophisticated. I caught a glimpse of her eyes. They were smoky. Don't ask me what I mean by smoky. I can't tell you. But if you saw them and I asked you to describe them, you'd say they were beautiful . . . and smoky.

I was into my second or third vodka and tonic – maybe fourth – when this skinny, tall, red-headed dude got up from the table he was sitting at and approached the beautiful, smoky-eyed brunette. He asked her if he could buy her a drink. Well, actually he didn't ask; he told he was going to buy her a drink.

"Hey, Beautiful, I'm gonna buy you a drink!" he said.

"No, thank you," she responded.

"Come on, let me buy you a drink. I wanna sit and talk to you, get to know you!" he said with a little more force this time.

"No, thank you; I'm not looking for company," the lovely young lady insisted.

"What the hell is wrong with you? Is there something about me you don't like? I just want to sit and talk"

I was on my feet when the tall redhead spat the words *wrong with you,* and approached him just as he arrived at *sit and talk.*

"The lady said she's not interested in having a drink with you, so go back to your table and sit down," I told him.

I was close enough to get a strong whiff of his halitosis.

I wasn't certain what to expect at that moment. I was surprised when he turned on his heels and returned to his table.

Moments later, this heavy-set dude with thinning hair and a square jaw walked into the joint and as he approached the bar, I spotted him staring at me. Then he approached and said, "You look familiar as hell. Where have I seen you?"

He sat down to my right, ordered another drink and one for me.

"I don't know," I said, "You from around here?"

"Just recently," he said. "I moved here last week from Lawrence."

"You're not a fight fan, are you?" I asked. "I did quite a bit of fighting up in Lawrence, Frost Arena."

"Sure, that's it," he said. "You're Rocky . . . Rocky . . . ah . . ."

"Scarpati," I finished the name for him.

"That's right, Rocky Scarpati. Good to meet you. I used to love to watch you fight."

He told me his name was Bill Jenkins and he was a state cop. Most recently out of the Middleboro barracks."

Then – oomph – I felt an elbow into my ribs.

The tall ugly redhead – did I mention to you before he was ugly? – was now on the stool to my left and had stuck an elbow into my side.

"You know, you're an asshole," he said. "Let's take this outside."

He kind of caught me off guard. When I didn't respond right away, Jenkins said to me, "Go ahead; go with him!"

I shrugged my shoulders, nodded to the tall redhead and slipped off my barstool. The redhead led the way out the door with a wide, obnoxious stride.

As soon as we got to the sidewalk and the barroom door closed behind us, Red wheeled around, put me into a headlock and threw us both to the cement. Shit, that could have been embarrassing as hell if anyone was there to see it. But, fortunately, there was no one there to witness it. When we hit the sidewalk, it jarred me free of the headlock and I quickly scampered to my feet. Hell, I couldn't believe Red wanted to wrestle. That was like bringing a knife to a gunfight.

On my feet now and squared off in front of the dude, I feinted a right hand to his body. Just like I had done so many times to so many opponents in the ring. And just like I had done so many times to so many scabs when I was walking a union picket line. And like I had done to a cop or two here or there. Red's guard came down and I unleashed my legendary and patented left hook and caught Big Red on the sweet spot on the side of his jaw. He went down and the back of his head cracked against the barroom door. He laid there silent, his eyes still and I was afraid I had killed the bastard. But then I noticed his eyes move and he moaned.

At that moment the barroom door was forced slightly open against Red's body. Bill Jenkins had to step over Big Red to get outside. Right then, the timing couldn't have been more perfect.

There I was, standing over the fallen bully with my fist clenched just like the famous photograph of Muhammad Ali standing over a fallen Sonny Liston. Jenkins flashed his badge at Red and told him to "get the fuck outta here."

And you're not going to believe what happened. Old Red got to his feet and ran – yes ran – down Montello Street.

When I returned to the barroom the conquering hero, the beautiful brunette with the captivating smoky eyes smiled - a warm, sincere, infectious smile – and said, "Thank you."

I thought of asking her if I could buy her a drink. But wouldn't that make me no better than Big Red? I mean, the lady said she didn't want company. But, if she told me, "No thanks," she didn't want me buying her a drink, unlike Big Red, I wouldn't have insisted. I would have taken no for an answer. Yeah, I thought of asking if I could buy her a drink, but I didn't. I know this sounds hokey as hell, but it's the truth. I actually asked myself what The Lone Ranger would do. So I finished the vodka and tonic I was drinking when Bill Jenkins came in. I finished the one Jenkins bought for me and I left. I only regretted that I didn't have a silver bullet to hand the beautiful young lady.

CHAPTER 27

...EVERYBODY'S GONNA SEE!

I told you before how I once went to trial for a murder I didn't commit. That's one thing, sitting in a courtroom, watching the government's case unfold in front of you. Stressful as all hell. But it's quite another thing to have some dude on trial for a murder you *actually did* commit and you're not there to hear what's happening. You just don't know if somehow the scales of justice are going to tilt in the right direction. Your direction. Waiting for Audacity to return from the Providence courthouse Wednesday, I asked myself over and over again: Which was worse, on trial for a murder you didn't commit or not there for a murder you *did* commit? And the answer was always the same. Not being there was definitely worse, much worse.

It seemed like forever, but actually was quite a bit earlier than I expected, when Audacity stepped off *The Examiner* elevator. It had been raining and she was wearing a sleek, sexy black raincoat. It reminded me of the raincoat Eva Green was wearing that unforgettable night at *The Ambassador*. The night she picked me up and brought me to *The Palace Hotel* to walk into the brass-knuckled fist of none other than Maurice diMontiferro. This particular day at *The Examiner*, Audacity's makeup was running fiercely.

I didn't wait. I got up from my desk and rushed over to greet her. All the while, trying to act like I wasn't rushing to greet her.

"Did the prosecution rest its case?" I asked.

"Yup. And so did the defense."

"Really? Did Maurice diMontiferro take the stand?"

"Yup, he certainly did."

"And what did he say?"

"I'll tell you in a few minutes. I've got to go to the ladies' room and fix my makeup. Or didn't you notice it's all over my face?"

As soon as Audacity returned – ten minutes later after the facial repairs – I eagerly asked her again: "So what did diMontiferro say?"

Audacity hesitated. Gave me a very weird look. Cocked her head and blurted: "He said you did it."

I literally lost my breath. It was exactly like the finals of the New England Golden Gloves when a muscular, dark-skinned ringer by the name of Henry Colon planted a sweeping left hook into my gut and totally stole my breath. About 10 to 12 seconds into the first round. What kind of a name is *Henry* for a fighter, anyhow?

I was standing there, attempting not to give the impression that I was gasping for my next breath, when Audacity added: "Hey, I'm just kidding. But you lost all the color in your face when I said it."

I ignored the accusation. If, in fact, it was an accusation.

The audacity of her!

"What did he say?"

"He said his former girlfriend, Eva . . . Eva . . . ah . . ."

"Eva Green," I provided Audacity with the last name.

"Yeah, Eva Green, why, do you *know* her?"

"No, you mentioned her name previously," I said.

Audacity thought about that a moment, but didn't say a damn thing. Just shrugged her shoulders. It was if she didn't recall mentioning the name Eva Green earlier. And, to be perfectly honest, I didn't either.

"Well, he said his former girlfriend, Eva Green, did it. Or must have done it. He said it couldn't have been anyone but her."

"Why?"

"I'll tell you later," Audacity said. "I want to get this story written. Then you can take me out for a drink and I'll answer all your questions."

That didn't do a thing to relax my anxiety.

Audacity wasn't decked out to the nines like she was the previous day when she was going out with her uncle. Now she looked slightly more like a newspaper reporter than a hooker. Although a particularly attractive newspaper reporter. Attractive and sexy. Yeah, she still wore a rather sexy miniskirt - I don't think she ever wore any clothes that went below her knees – but she was also wearing a blouse buttoned up to the vicinity of her neck. That, on the other hand, was unusual.

After Audacity finished pounding out her story of the day's events in the Providence courthouse, she retrieved her raincoat and asked where we were going for a nightcap.

"I don't know; where do you want to go?" I asked.

"Capeway," she said.

When I didn't answer her right away and probably gave her a questioning look, she added: ". . .you don't have to buy me dinner; we can just have a drink."

I breathed a sigh of relief – I mean, my finances were strained more than a little bit since my breakup with my wife and then with Barbara - but with all the enthusiasm of a wet dish rag I added: "I could buy you dinner."

She grinned broadly and didn't skip a beat before responding.

"OK!" she said.

Shit! I wasn't expecting that!

I drove us to *Capeway* in my noisy, old VW Karmann Ghia.

"So what did Maurice diMontiferro say on the witness stand today?" I asked as the windshield wipers clip-clopped in a disjointed rhythm in front of us.

"I'm telling you, what a big lug!" she exclaimed. "What a big, dumb lug! He's stupid!"

"Yeah, I figured that, but what did he say?"

"He said . . . what's her name? Eva Green did it."

"Just like that, he came right out and said Eva Green did it!' statement of fact, just like that, 'Eva Green did it?'" I asked.

"Yup, just like that, statement of fact," Audacity repeated. "The prosecutor, Peter Constable, objected vehemently. And, of course, Judge Carlotta Abernathy sustained the objection."

"Abernathy turned to the witness and said, 'You can't come out and say that someone did it unless you saw her do it and you're testifying that you saw her do it.' do you understand that, Mr. diMontiferro?"

"'Yes, I understand,' diMontiferro replied. 'But she did it.'
Abernathy asked: "Did you see her kill Mr. Macrillo?"

"No . . . but she did it!"

"Abernathy opened her mouth to respond, but she just sort of shook her head. Without attempting to push Maurice any further, she simply said, 'Let the record reflect that Mr. Constable's objection to the witness's assertion that Eva Green *did it*, was sustained.'"

"'Why do you *think* that Ms. Green *did it?*' The defense attorney . . . ah . . . Richard Egbert asked.

"diMontiferro said he was being framed. He said that someone called him in his apartment and hung up after one ring. That was a signal that only Angel Macrillo, Eva Green and he knew about and used. When any of them got the signal, one ring then the hang up, he – or she – would know to report to the bungalow at 1025 Seacrest Ave."

My mind whirled back to that nightmarish scene in the bungalow. I had a vague memory of Eva going to the telephone. Dialing a number. Hanging up. No, it was more than a vague memory. I remembered. I remembered it vividly.

"Ten, twenty five Seacrest Avenue, that was the address of the shooting?" I asked.

"Yup, that was the address," Audacity confirmed.

"Sounds high class," I noted.

"Not high class; just a bungalow in the woods," she responded.

"So, anyway, diMontiferro was saying there were only three people who could have given the signal to report to the bungalow. One was Angelo. He couldn't have done it; he was dead. diMontiferro didn't call himself. So that left, Eva – what's her name – Eva Green. She must have made the call. She made it to set him up for the murder, he claimed."

"So why did they have this signal to report to the bungalow, anyhow?" I asked.

"diMontiferro claimed that Angelo was paranoid. He was into all sorts of illegal shit and was always paranoid that the cops had his phone tapped. If ever the three of them had to communicate, he wanted it done in person. And he didn't want to tip the cops off to the fact that they'd be communicating. So he had this system worked out that would get them together."

Audacity smiled.

"It was kind of cute. On cross-examination, Peter Constable asked the defendant why he, Angel and Eva Green would have to communicate without the cops or anyone knowing they were communicating. Were they into illegal activities?

"diMontiferro said he was going to have to plead the fifth to that.

"'I don't want to say nothin' that's gonna criminate myself,' he testified."

"When the judge told him he didn't get to pick and choose what he was going to testify about; either he was going to answer all the questions asked of him or none at all, diMontiferro said: 'OK, Angel, Eva and me, we did some shit that I ain't particularly proud of, but it was mostly Eva and Angel that did the heavy shit; I didn't do any of the felonious stuff!'

"You know, after hearing diMontiferro's testimony, a lot of Constable's cross-examination of previous witnesses made more sense."

"Oh, yeah," I asked, "how so?"

"When the cops received the telephone call about the shooting, Constable made a big deal about the cop's description of the person calling. It was female. The voice was extremely muffled, like whoever called had a handkerchief or something around the mouthpiece of the telephone to disguise it. I can just see Constable now arguing that Eva Green made the call. She got lucky, however, when diMontiferro picked up the gun and was standing over the body when the cops arrived."

"Sounds pretty elaborate to me," I replied. "And pretty unlikely. The timing is too bazaar.

"Motive?" I asked. "Did diMontiferro mention a motive?"

"He said Angel had beaten the shit out of her. He said Eva had told him that she was going to take care of Angel. When he asked her what she meant about that, she responded: 'You'll see; Everybody's gonna see!'"

CHAPTER 28
ALWAYS THE BRIDESMAID. . .

"You know what was really weird?" Audacity asked. "Eva Green, an extremely beautiful woman, by the way, totally beautiful, was in the courtroom listening to all of this. And then Richard Egbert asked diMontiferro if Eva Green was in court. He said, "She sure is," and pointed toward her. She didn't react at all. Totally stoic. An ice lady.

"After diMontiferro testified, Richard Egbert rested the case for the defense. Eva Green got Constable's attention, who begged the court's indulgence and conferred with her briefly at the railing. Then he asked the judge to break for the day. He said the prosecution would be presenting rebuttal witnesses, but he needed time to confer with them.

"Egbert said, 'Hey, wait a minute,' this was the first he was hearing about any additional prosecution witnesses.

"The judge said she'd not only break for the day, she'd recess over Thursday and Friday also. She told Constable to jot down the names and their contact information on a piece of paper and provide them to Egbert. That would give the defense a long weekend to prepare for their testimony."

"Who's Constable going to have testify, Eva Green?" I asked.

"I don't know. He didn't say. But he did say *witnesses* so I'd expect it will be more than one."

I swerved into *Capeway* parking lot and splashed through the puddles there. We went inside and ordered prime ribs. Damn near broke me. Hey, I couldn't use a credit card. My only credit card had maxed out the month before.

After dinner, I drove Audacity back to her car. I didn't even suggest getting a room – well, I never could have afforded it anyway – or going back to my room although, I've got to admit, that thought did enter my mind. But I never propositioned Audacity about it because I was anxious to get to the *Palace Hotel.* Alone. Certainly, it figured, tonight, of all nights, Eva Green would be attempting to reach me by phone. I didn't have a telephone in my room. The places Eva would think to reach me would be at work or the *Palace Hotel.*

But I never got a call. The only thing I got that night was drunk.

The next morning, I woke up with a battalion of soldiers marching through my head. But there was no way I was staying home this particular day. I loaded up on oxycodone and floated into work. How the hell could Eva Green leave me hanging like that? What the hell did she say to Peter Constable to make him ask for a break in the action? Was she going to testify herself? Come on, what could she say? Was she going to say I did the dastardly deed all by myself? Hang me out to dry?

Unbelievable, after getting back to my room drunk, I couldn't get to sleep. Well, sometimes booze can do that to you. When I finally got to sleep, I overslept. But I wasn't going to miss work this particular day. I skipped breakfast, skipped a shower, didn't even put on a tie – screw the dress code – and arrived approximately the same time I did most days.

Still, Managing Editor Hugh Beckerman greeted me with a resounding, "Good afternoon, Mr. Scarpati, so nice of you to award us with your presence."

When I sat down at my desk, I discovered Eva had already called and left me a message. One line.

"Don't worry; everything's under control."

That was it. "Don't worry; everything's under control." That was it; nothing more.

So, what do you do with yourself when you're facing the longest weekend of your life? I mean, my fate was in somebody's hands. Whose hands? Eva's? And she leaves me a five-word message telling me not to worry. So why wasn't I supposed to worry? "Everything is under control," that's why.

Yeah, that explained it.

So, there wasn't going to be anything happening in the courtroom that day. Or Friday. And obviously nothing Saturday or Sunday. OK, what do you do on a long tumultuous weekend when your fate – hell, the freedom for the rest of your life – is hanging in the balance?

Obviously. . .

. . . You drink!

As soon as I got out of work mid-afternoon that Thursday, I started out at *The Ambassador*. Then I headed on over to *The Palace Hotel* to continue the goal of getting drunk as a skunk. And then about 7, 8 or 9 p.m. – who the hell knows? – I dropped into *Bernies*. I used to do a lot of drinking at *Bernies*. Not so much recently. It was a particularly friendly establishment located on a tiny dead-end street near the center of Brockton.

I glided in and was pleased to see Sherry behind the bar. Sherry, the sexiest brunette this side of Chicago was built like the proverbial brick shithouse.

I once had an after-closing-hours rendezvous with Sherry in an office over a gymnasium behind the bar. Shit, I thought to myself, I certainly could use another of those after-closing-hours rendezvous with that particular goddess right now.

"Hello, stranger," Sherry said with a hint of a smile. "Haven't seen you in a while."

"Guilty as charged," I responded.

She flashed a smile.

A warm, sensuous, sexy smile.

177

"I was beginning to think my performance was so disappointing that you decided to give up drinking," she quipped.

"Not at all. Furthest thing from my mind. I was totally captivated. In fact, the thought of an encore has crossed my mind on numerous occasions."

"Sorry," she said, as she placed her left hand on the bar in front of me. "You waited too long. I'm engaged."

I immediately gazed down at the ring on her finger.

"Break the engagement," I mused. "I'll buy you a bigger one."

Nodding to her left, she said: "That's my fiancé, sitting at the end of the bar."

I withdrew my hand, but not in a hurry and not until I gave it a little squeeze. Then I casually gazed to my right to take a gander at the lucky feller. He didn't look so tough. Maybe I should have massaged Sherry's hand a little longer.

"What's your pleasure?" the stranger sitting next to me asked in a booming voice.

He was bulky, clean-shaven and clean-cut, his brown hair parted on the left side like a school kid's.

"Let me buy you a drink," he added.

"I'll have a vodka and tonic," I said, which may have been totally unnecessary. I was confident Sherry knew what I drank.

"And give me another one," the stranger next to me told her.

He was drinking a Miller.

Out of the bottle, no glass.

He stuck out his hand, saying, "Bob Zebras, you've probably heard of me."

"I can't say that I have," I said as I shook his hand.

He was one of these characters who tried to impress you with a handshake that was a vice.

I wasn't particularly impressed and didn't bother to mention my name.

"I'm a state cop, a lieutenant-detective," Zebras noted. Obviously very proud of the title; "I'm very well known around Brockton."

I didn't particularly know what to say, so I didn't say anything.

"I'm not on the clock right now, I'm not here officially," Zebras spouted, "but you might say I'm getting the lay of the land. Hey, after all, a state police detective's work is never done. He's never totally off duty. He sees something or knows something ain't right, he makes it right."

I had no goddamn idea how to respond to that.

So I didn't.

"I'm getting the lay of the land," Zebras repeated. "I'm gonna bust Bernie."

Zebras was obviously referring to the owner of the establishment in which we were drinking. I mean, it was, after all, named *Bernie's*.

"You know, Bernie's a bookie?" Zebras said both as a statement of fact and a question. Hell, the whole City of Brockton knew Bernie was a bookie, but I wasn't going to give Sherlock Holmes the satisfaction of either confirming or denying that I knew. So, I simply took a gulp of my vodka and tonic.

"I wonder why Bernie isn't here tonight. The barmaid – what's her name, Sherry? – probably called him and told him to stay away."

Hmmm. I once asked Bernie how he got away with it. You know, being a bookie. Bob Zebras was right. Everybody in Brockton knew Bernie was a bookie. Bernie told me the answer was simple; he said he paid off the cops.

I guess Bob Zebras wasn't on his payroll.

I got Sherry's attention, ordered another drink and told her to give the good detective another beer.

And the next thing I knew Zebras was challenging me to a game of pool. The loser, he said, would set up the bar.

Well, you know – and I know – that my finances weren't all that wonderful at that point in my life and I wouldn't be carrying enough money to set up the bar, but that was no problem. No, not because I was sure I was going to win. I was no kind of pool hustler. I barely knew which end of the stick to put out over the table. But, when I drank at *Bernies,* I ran a tab. I could afford to lose and it wouldn't hurt until it was time to pay the tab.

A funny thing happened. Zebras took out his piece and laid it on the edge of the table while we shot our game of pool. Made a very big production out of it, too. Didn't just set it down. Put it there with a bit of a thud. So everyone in the gin joint would notice. Didn't seem much like standard police procedure to me.

Like I said, there was no way in hell I even casually resembled Minnesota Fats or Fast Eddie Felson. But, lo and behold, I won the game. Bob Zebras set up the bar. First, he made a spectacle of reholstering his piece. Made certain everyone got a gander.

I don't remember exactly how we got into it, but moments later we were again sitting at the bar and Zebras was telling me how tough he was. I guess he really didn't need any special transition into the subject, he just liked to brag.

"I can't tell you how much confidence it gives me knowing that when I walk into a joint, any joint, I'm the toughest guy there," Zebras boasted.

"Ah-ha," I said, trying not to sound overly impressed.

"What's the matter?" he asked. "You don't think so? Hmm. Maybe you don't think I'm the toughest guy here? Maybe you think you're pretty tough? Is that it? You think you're tough? You think you can beat me?"

Years later, in a debate, Hillary Clinton said something to the effect of, "when they take the low road; we take the high road." Well, I had her beat by years and years. While Zebras was sitting there sounding like a braggart and an asshole, I came across soft spoken and modest."

"Well, I used to do a little fighting," I noted.

"You mean in the ring?" he asked.

"Yeah, I used to be pretty good."

"Well, that's no big deal," he said. "I could still beat the shit out of you."

I just sort of shrugged my shoulders and took a sip of my drink.

"You ever fight in the Golden Gloves?" Zebras asked.

"Yeah, I finished runner up."

"Always the bridesmaid, never the bride, huh?" he spat.

"I wouldn't say *always* the bridesmaid. I only fought in The gloves' once. I finished runner up."

"*Always* the bridesmaid," Zebras repeated.

You know I've met a few people since who know Bob Zebras. Quite a few people, actually, who have been acquainted with him. And they all said he was a helluva nice guy. I couldn't see it. He struck me as being a raving asshole. I don't know; maybe it was just when he was drinking.

"You think you can beat me; is that what you're sayin'?" Zebras spouted. "Come on, there's a gym out back. We'll just go out back there and see how tough you are?"

"Well, yeah, there's a gym back there; but there aren't any gloves," I noted.

"What kind of a gym, is it?" he sounded aghast. "What kind of a gym has no boxing gloves?"

"It's a boxing gym, alright, but Bernie doesn't supply the gloves," I explained. "Everybody brings their own gloves."

"Goddamn it, what kind of gym is that?" Zebras repeated.

"I'll tell you what, give me a few minutes. I'll drive home and get a couple pair of 16-ounce gloves."

"Oh, yeah, you'll drive home and get them?"

"Yeah, I'll go get them."

"I'll drive you home to get them," Zebras bellowed.

CHAPTER 29

NO MAS

Zebras pulled up to a parking spot on Montello Street in front of the Bright Lights Café. I asked him what we were stopping there for. He merely responded, "Another drink."

OK.

The Bright Lights Café was where I did my best Lone Ranger impression and rescued a pretty damsel in distress. Then left before giving her the opportunity to demonstrate how much she appreciated it. When Zebras and I walked into the joint, I kind of hoped the beautiful young lady might be there.

She wasn't.

The bartender was different, too. When I walked in with Zebras, I don't think there was anyone there who had witnessed my previous heroics.

Zebras ordered me a vodka and tonic and himself a Miller.

The Bright Lights Café was extremely misnamed. There was one tiny, fluorescent sign outside and the inside was dark and dank.

Six minutes after our arrival, a meek, troubled young man with thick glasses stumbled through the front door, asking who owned the blue Ford that was parked out front.

"That would be me," Zebras boomed.

"I just sideswiped your car," the young man said, "I'm really sorry. I'll pay for the damage; I promise."

"You drunk?" Zebras barked. "You been drinking?"

"No, sir, I don't drink. I'll pay for the damage."

"Yeah, you don't drink; that's what they all say."

"OK, let's go out and have a look," Zebras responded. "Your insurance company will pay for it. You are insured, aren't you?"

"Yes, sir, I am. But that's what I wanted to ask you. I've had a couple of claims recently and I'm afraid I'll lose my insurance. I was hoping we could take care of it, just between us. You get an estimate of what it will cost to fix and I'll pay you."

"Let's take a look."

The damage was minimal.

"Let me see your license and registration," Zebras said. "OK, I'll find out what it's gonna cost and I'll be in touch. You can pay me directly; keep the insurance company out of this."

I was wondering why Zebras was being so contrite. I thought maybe he had lied to me and he wasn't off duty. Maybe he would have a tough time explaining what he was doing in the Bright Lights Café if he were on duty. Or maybe he was just being a decent guy. From the Bob Zebras I had observed up to that point, it seemed unlikely.

After I finished my vodka and tonic and Zebras took the last gulp of his Miller, we left the Bright Lights Café and, minutes later, we were pulling up to the *The Mission* on Legion Parkway.

"And what are we doing stopping here?" I asked.

"Another drink," Zebras responded.

Big George and his ol' Okie girlfriend, Sarah, were at the bar.

"Just the man I wanted to see," Big George boomed. "I went to trial today. Not guilty!"

"How the hell did. . ." I cut myself short before I said more. I mean, how the hell could old George be found not guilty after being apprehended sitting on his front lawn with a cash register drawer, counting the proceeds of his theft?

"How could I be found not guilty?" George finished the question for me. "Because I didn't do nothin'. I'm not guilty."

"Hey George, this is Bob Zebras. And this is Big George's girlfriend, Sarah," I introduced them.

"Zebras? Bob Zebras?" the name sounds familiar," George wondered out loud.

"He's a cop, a state cop," I said.

"See, I told you, everybody's heard of me," Zebras beamed.

"Yeah, that's it, that's where I know the name from," Big George agreed, sounding something less than thrilled.

Sarah reached out and touched my arm.

"The lawyer you got for George, Kevin Reddington, he was a magician. That's how George was found innocent."

Turning to me, Zebras noted: "You got him Reddington?"

When I proudly nodded, Zebras added, "Nothing but the best for Rocky Scarpati's friend, huh?"

"When we asked Kevin what we owed him," George said: "he told us 'Nothing at all, just take Rocky out to dinner sometime.'"

That was the last I ever heard about dinner. It was never brought up again. People who live on Green Street drink; they don't go to dinner. If Kevin had said buy Rocky a drink, George would have done it. A dinner? I'd never see one.

Finally, we stopped outside my apartment building on Green Street and I retrieved the boxing gloves. Zebras made some wise-ass comment about it being a "nice neighborhood" that I hung my hat in. And then we were walking back into Bernie's and, get this, the asshole had the nerve to invite everybody at the bar into the gym to watch him "beat the shit" out of me. There were quite a few folks at *Bernie's* on this particular Thursday night and the backroom became crowded, indeed.

We recruited Arnie, the jewel thief, to be the time keeper and Pete, the plumber, to be the referee.

John Higgins was going to be one judge and Bobby Littlefield, who once was accused of being a flasher, was the other. If the bout went the distance, the two judges and the referee would determine the winner. Without consulting me in advance, Zebras announced the loser would set the bar up for a round of drinks. I guess because I had agreed to pay for a round if I lost our pool match – and I didn't lose – Zebras felt comfortable suggesting I'd pay if I lost the fight.

We had agreed to slate the match for four, three-minute rounds, but as we entered the ring, Zebras bellowed, "Let's make it five, three-minute rounds."

"Yeah, whatever," I said, still being the modest combatant.

Then Zebras stepped forward, crowding my face and said to me – but loud enough for everyone to hear – "Don't go easy on me, kid, because, by God, I ain't gonna go easy on you!"

You know, I probably should have paid a little better heed to Bob's warning, but hell, I was the prize fighter, I was the one with all the experience at this kind of shit and I was good, goddamn straight, I knew I was good. But about 10 – maybe 15 seconds – into the fight he tagged me on the chin with a mighty right hand that sent my head reeling. I was knocked back to my heels and for the next few moments I felt like I was taking a lonely stroll along Queer Street.

Embarrassed? Yeah, I was goddamn embarrassed. But thanking my lucky stars that I didn't go down. That would have been totally unbearable!

I gritted my teeth. Tucked in my chin. And was now totally, 100 percent committed to taking the advice Bob Zebras had dealt out with such a cavalier attitude. I wasn't going to take it easy!

I stepped forward with my Sonny Liston jab. My bread and butter. Always had been. Always would be. A ramrod. Straight forward. Hard. Fast.

And then another.

Carbon copy of the first.

And then another.

His head snapped back.

And then again.

And again.

I dropped into a crouch.

Flicked out my right hand toward his body.

Just a flick.

Nothing behind it.

Just to get him to drop his guard.

Like I had done so many times throughout my boxing career.

Like I had done so many times in street fights.

Like I had done to the loudmouth that night recently at *The Bright Lights Café*.

Then I loaded up and threw everything I had into a devastating left hook to Zebras' head.

A mighty left hook.

My bread and butter.

Always had been.

Always will be.

It sent Bob Zebras reeling back on his heels.

And then I was back into my crouch.

I flicked out my right hand.

Just a flick.

Nothing more.

Just to get Zebras to drop his guard.

Then I leaped out of the crouch and threw a mighty left hook.

Again, my bread and butter.

Again, always had been.

Always would be.

It crashed into the side of Zebras' head.

He rocked back onto his heels and, I swear, he would have gone down if he hadn't plunged into the ropes, his right hand grabbing onto the top rope, keeping him upright.

As I shuffled forward for the kill, Zebras raised his left hand into the air and loudly proclaimed: "That's it, I'm done!"

Years later – actually, it was about four years later – I thought about that moment when I watched TV and saw Roberto Duran throw up his hands and proclaim, "No mas!" in his bout against Sugar Ray Leonard.

"No mas," loosely translated, means "No more."

Of course the whole world was watching when Roberto Duran surrendered in disgrace.

There was only a roomful of drinkers to witness Zebras' submission.

But I still loved it.

CHAPTER 30

BEWITCHED, BOTHERED AND BEWILDERED

After the longest weekend of my life – but one I hardly can remember; booze will do that to you – I called into work sick Monday morning. Well, not actually sick. I told whoever answered the phone that I couldn't make an appearance that particular day because I was *Bewitched, Bothered and Bewildered*. You can get away with that sort of shit when you're president of the union. I'm not entirely certain what I had in mind when I said it. It just had a nice ring to it. Actually, Richard Rogers probably had a much better idea of the meaning behind it when he penned the song.

The thing is, I couldn't go to work at *The Examiner* and even begin to concentrate on my work when my fate – my freedom, my very existence – was hanging in a Providence courtroom. For all I knew, Eva Green was going to take the witness stand and tell the world that I had plugged Angelo "Angel" Macrillo all by myself. I had to go to Providence to see and hear what was happening.

After I walked into the courthouse, Eva sidled up beside me and attempted to talk to me without giving the appearance she was talking to me. Out of the side of her mouth, she asked: "What are you doing here?"

She made it abundantly clear that she wasn't happy to see me there.

"I came to find out what's happening," I responded in a hushed tone.

"I told you everything was under control," she protested.

"Yeah what was that supposed to mean? For all I know, you're gonna get on the witness stand and sell me out."

"I'm not going to testify," Eva said, surprising the hell out of me. "What makes you think I was?"

"Because I heard you had a little conference with the assistant DA and afterwards he told the court he had rebuttal witnesses."

"Yeah true, rebuttal witnesses. But not me," Eva sounded a bit stressed.

"Besides, I'd never say you did it," she added. "I love you."

I wondered how that could even vaguely be true. For all intents and purposes, Eva barely knew me. I was never one to believe in love at first sight. Not true love.

But I then told her, "I love you, too."

I didn't know how that could be true, either.

She gave my hand a gentle squeeze.

Minutes later, inside the courtroom, Judge Abernathy noted: "Mr. Constable, I understand you have rebuttal witnesses."

"Yes, I do, your honor. The state calls Sister Agatha."

Sister Agatha sashayed into the courtroom in her habit. How anybody can sashay into a room in full nun garb is beyond me, but Sister Agatha managed it in spades. The curves to her body were pretty well hidden due to the outfit, but I just knew that this was the kind of chick old Tony Lombardi would say was "built like a brick shithouse without a brick outta place."

From where I was seated, the most breathtaking thing about Sister Agatha was her eyes. I know I told you in the past that Eva Green had the deepest, most beautiful eyes I had ever seen. I was wrong. Sister Agatha's were deeper, more beautiful. They were more beautiful and, I'm certain, more dangerous than the deep blue sea. Her eyes yearned to reach out, pull you in and drown you.

You may be thinking and telling yourself right now that I should go straight to hell for having such thoughts about a nun. Or, at least, for expressing them out loud. But I think the real sin is that some chick so outrageously ravishing would ever become a nun.

Everyone in the courtroom soon learned Sister Agatha wasn't a full-fledged nun. Yes, she had earned the title "sister" and she explained the difference between a "sister' and a "nun," but I wasn't really paying attention. I was still sort of spellbound. She said something to the effect that she was a nun in training.

Sister Agatha testified she had known Eva Green for a very long time. They had met in high school and remained friends afterwards. And, most importantly, they had met for dinner on the evening of Tuesday, November 25, 1975, the date Angel Macrillo was murdered. And then Eva, Sister Agatha and a Sister Therese went out to a late-night movie. And then to donut shop for coffee during the early morning hours. So obviously, it was clear to one and all in the courtroom that Eva couldn't have been home murdering Macrillo if she was out with Sisters Agatha and Therese.

Asked by Assistant District Attorney Constable what movie they had seen, the Sister replied: THE ROCKY HORROR PICTURE SHOW."

Constable asked his witness how she could be certain it was November 25, 1975, that she went to the movies with Eva and Sister Therese.

"Because Eva Green called me the next day to tell me her boyfriend had been murdered the previous night."

During cross-examination, Richie Egbert noted, "THE ROCKY HORROR PICTURE SHOW, it sounds like a cartoon," and asked, "was it a cartoon?"

"No, it wasn't," Sister Agatha responded.

"What kind of movie was it?" Egbert asked in his raspy voice.

"A musical."

"A musical?" Egbert repeated in amazement. "Well, it was more than just a musical, wasn't it?"

"I guess so."

"What other kind of movie was it."

"Well, I guess you could call it a horror movie," Sister Agatha responded. "Or a comedy; I guess it was sort of a horror and a comedy. And a musical."

"Very unusual combination, Egbert noted, "a musical, a horror movie and a comedy?"

"Yes, very unusual," the witness agreed.

"Tell me about it," Richie suggested.

"Tell you about it?"

"Your Honor," I object, Constable interrupted, "this is getting pretty far afield."

"No, I'll allow it," the judge ruled.

"Tell me about the plot," Egbert urged.

"Well, let me see. . . it was about a young couple – I think they were engaged – and their car broke down near a country house – well, it looked like a castle. The couple went there to ask to use the telephone to get some help. There were a whole bunch of people in outlandish costumes in the country house, the castle. They were there for some kind of convention."

"What kind of convention?" Egbert asked.

"Umm."

"Wasn't it an annual Transylvanian convention?" Egbert suggested.

"Yes, I guess that was it."

"Who was the head of the household?"

"A very strange man."

"What was his name?'

"I don't know; something very weird like Franks and Beans or something like that."

"If I suggested to you that he was named Frank N. Furter, would that jog your memory?"

"Yes, I guess that's right."

"Tell me about Frank N. Furter."

"Your Honor, I have to object again," the prosecutor spoke up with a hint of pleading in his voice.

"Overruled," Abernathy responded. "This is quite entertaining."

"Thank you, Your Honor," this from Richie Egbert. "Sister Agatha, tell me about Frank N. Furter."

"Well, he was a scientist."

Egbert urged the witness to go on, saying: "And . . ."

"Well, I guess you'd call him a mad scientist."

"And . . ." Egbert again.

"He dances and sings."

"And. . ."

"He's an alien."

"Sister Agatha," Egbert barked, "isn't Frank N. Furter also a transvestite?"

"Umm, yes; I guess he is."

"And isn't the couple who came to his door seduced separately by Frank N. Furter?

"Yes, they are."

"What was THE ROCKY HORROR PICTURE SHOW rated?" Richie asked.

"I don't know; I didn't pay attention to its rating."

"Was it Triple X rated?"

"Oh, no, I certainly don't think so."

"Was it X rated?"

"No."

"Was it R rated?"

"Yes, it was R rated."

"So you did pay attention to the rating," Egbert alleged.

"Your Honor," Constable piped up.

"Yes, the jurors will disregard the defense attorney's comment," Abernathy responded.

"Why was THE ROCKY HORROR PICTURE SHOW given an R rating?" Egbert asked.

"I don't know. I suppose it was due to sexual content."

"What was the sexual content?"

There was a long hesitation from the witness. She gazed at the judge as if she wanted to be rescued from having to respond.

She wasn't rescued.

"Answer the question," Judge Abernathy instructed.

"Some of the characters were receiving fellatio," the sister said.

I thought I detected a slight blush from Sister Agatha during that response.

"Who suggested going to see THE ROCKY HORROR PICTURE SHOW?" Egbert asked.

"Eva did," she responded. "She said she had heard a lot about it and really wanted to see it."

Then, before another question was asked, Sister Agatha added: "I didn't know a about the movie before we saw it."

"If you had known what it was about, would you have gone to see it?"

"Oh, no, I never would have gone."

"Even though your good friend, Eva Green, said she really wanted to see it?"

"I never would have gone," Sister Agatha insisted.

"Tell me, what did you think of Faye Dunaway's performance in that movie?"

"Objection," Peter Constable shouted.

"I don't remember Faye Dunaway being in the movie," she responded, oblivious to the objection.

"I'll withdraw the objection," Constable noted, relieved that the witness hadn't fallen for the apparent trap.

"Mr. Constable, do you have any other witnesses?" Judge Abernathy asked after Sister Agatha was excused from the courtroom.

"Yes, Your Honor," the prosecution calls Sister Therese."

When Sister Therese, also wearing nuns' garb, shuffled into the courtroom, you got the strong impression that she would have benefitted greatly from the use of a walker. She was probably a good

30 to 40 years Sister Agatha's senior and, to be perfectly honest, those 30 to 40 years hadn't been all that gentle to her.

During direct examination, Sister Therese, who we learned was a full-fledged nun, confirmed everything Sister Agatha had said, right down to early morning coffee at the donut shop.

After Peter Constable completed his questioning, Judge Abernathy invited Richie Egbert to begin his cross.

Richie sat at the defense table, slightly slouched, his hands folded in front of him.

When he didn't move for a long moment, the judge urged, "Mr. Egbert?"

"Sister Therese," Egbert finally said. "I have only one question."

A long pause.

"Did you enjoy the movie?"

There was a loud snicker from one person in the courtroom. Out-and-out laughter from a couple of others.

So much so that the judge tapped her gavel.

This time, there was more than a hint of a blush from the witness. Sister Therese turned red – bright, bright red!

"No!" she responded rather indignantly.

CHAPTER 31

12 MINUTES

I could breathe a lot easier after hearing the testimony of sisters Agatha and Therese. I was more relaxed than I had been in a long time when I took Audacity to lunch at a hamburger joint around the corner from the courthouse. Judge Abernathy called for the lunch break after the sisters' testimony and said closing arguments would take place after lunch. I asked Audacity not to mention seeing me at the trial when she returned to *The Examiner*.

"Why, did you call in sick?" she asked.

"Nope," I boasted, "I called in bewitched, bothered and bewildered, but Hugh Beckerman probably interpreted that as my being sick."

For the first time in weeks, I felt relaxed and carefree, like the guillotine's blade that had been hanging over my head had been removed. That feeling of euphoria lasted until after lunch when Richie Egbert got into his closing argument on behalf of Maurice "The Hulk" diMontiferro. Then my feeling of relief disappeared in a New York minute. Damn, Egbert was good. Too goddamn good.

". . . You have to pay attention to the details," Richie told jurors shortly after he had begun his closing.

"We know Pawtucket police received a telephone call reporting the shooting at Seacrest Avenue at precisely 10:33 p.m. How do we know that? Police keep records of 911 calls.

197

"And we know from the testimony of the officers who responded to the scene, that they arrived at 10:45. That's 12 minutes after the report of the gunshot. Twelve minutes, a very long time."

Richie Egbert looked at his watch and for no apparent reason, told jurors, "it's now 1:16."

"We know the time between the shooting and the time officers arrived at the scene, was quite a bit greater than 12 minutes. The woman who purportedly heard the gunfire had to drive to a phone booth to make the 911 call. The bungalow where the murder took place was out in the woods; there were no pay phones readily available.

I never remembered stopping at a pay phone!

Egbert glanced at his watch.

"So we can easily expect that the time between the gunfire and the time in which it was reported was much more like 20 minutes. At a minimum. But, let's give the prosecution the benefit of the doubt. Let's say it was only 12 minutes between the time of the gunshot and the time it was reported.

"If Mr. diMontiferro was the gunman, if he did the shooting, what was he doing in the 12 minutes before police arrived at the scene?"

Egbert glanced at his watch.

"What was he doing, merely standing there and waiting for police to arrive?

"Nab him in the act?

"Holding what the prosecution in this trial loves to refer to as *the smoking gun?*

"When police arrived, Mr. diMontiferro was standing in precisely the exact spot the fatal shot was fired from.

"Twelve minutes later.

"Nothing better to do?

"Than stand there waiting for police to arrive?"

Another glance at his watch.

"Maybe he ate a sandwich? Ate a sandwich while he was deciding what to do with the body?

"The murder weapon was introduced into evidence.

"You've heard the testimony. There was one set of fingerprints.

"Mr. diMontiferro's.

"How likely is that?

"Wouldn't you think that other people would have handled the gun?

"You've heard the testimony . . . How fingerprints can last for days, months, years?

"Wouldn't you think that there'd be more than one set of fingerprints on the gun? Someone from the store where the weapon was purchased?

A glance at the watch.

"I'll tell you why there was only one set of prints on *the smoking gun.*

"Because whoever framed Mr. diMontiferro wiped the weapon clean before my client arrived. My client arrived on the scene, saw the victim sprawled on the floor, picked up the gun rather absentmindedly and held it. And then police arrived.

"Almost instantaneously. Otherwise, Mr. diMontiferro wouldn't still be standing there, holding the murder weapon, looking like a fool. Murderers don't stand around for 12 minutes – more than 12minutes – waiting for police to respond to the scene of the crime and arrest them."

"We don't have to prove to you who wiped off the murder weapon. We don't have to prove to you who framed Mr. diMontiferro. All we have to do is convince you that there is reasonable doubt my client committed the crime. And, if we do that, it is your responsibility to find Mr. diMontiferro not guilty."

Another glance at the watch by the defense attorney.

"I would suggest to you that the time element alone should give you reasonable doubt that Mr. diMontiferro committed the crime. He's not going to shoot Angelo Macrillo and then stand there waiting. . . waiting. . . waiting for police to arrive and arrest him.

"No, it's not our responsibility to prove to you who shot the victim and framed the defendant. Certainly Mr. diMontiferro attempted to do that when he testified on his own behalf. He told you it was Angelo Macrillo's lover, Eva Green, who did the dastardly deed. She certainly had the motive. Angelo Macrillo was an abusive boyfriend. He was brutalizing Ms. Green and his attacks were escalating. Certainly she was in fear for her life.

"But then, of course, you heard the testimony from Sister Agatha and Sister Therese. They said it couldn't have been Eva Green who committed the murder because they were with Ms. Green when the shooting took place. And, obviously, they wouldn't lie to you. Two women of the cloth wouldn't take an oath on the Holy Bible, no less, and then lie to you. . .

". . . Would they?

"If you believe Mr. diMontiferro's testimony that he was framed – and let me suggest to you, that you should – then it had to be Eva Green who framed him. Why should you believe Mr. diMontiferro was framed? Because it has the ring of truth. My client gets a telephone call – one ring – and he answers the phone. One ring. That's his signal to hightail it to the Seacrest Avenue house. And that's how he's so certain it was Eva Green who made the call. Only three people knew about the signal: the deceased, Eva Green and himself.

"When he arrives, he finds Angelo Macrillo's body sprawled, his head on the bathroom floor, his feet in the bedroom. He picks up the weapon absent-mindedly and then the police come barging into the bungalow. In an instant. Mr. diMontiferro wasn't standing there for 12 minutes – more than 12 minutes, much more than 12 minutes, I suggest to you - waiting for them.

"But Sister Agatha and Sister Therese wouldn't lie.

"Would they?

"Just because the witnesses were nuns, just because they were wearing habits, doesn't mean that their testimony should be held to any less scrutiny than anybody else's. And, so I ask you, did their testimony have the ring of truth? Does it seem likely that two God-fearing women would go see a movie about a transvestite who performs fellatio on any Tom, Dick, Alice or Harry who happens to knock on his door?

"Sister Agatha testified that she didn't know what the movie was about before she went to see it.

"How many people go to movies they know absolutely nothing about?

"And why, when she saw what is was about, didn't she get up and leave the theater?

"That's certainly what any reasonable person would expect an individual wearing a nun's habit to do?

"And what about Sister Therese?

"I'm certain all of you noted how crimson Sister Therese's complexion turned when I asked simply if she enjoyed the movie. I suggest that she would have left the theater; she would not have sat through THE ROCKY HORROR PICTURE SHOW – clad in her full nun's habit – once she saw what the movie was about.

"And then accompany Eva Green to an all-night donut shop?"

At this point, Richie Egbert talked about the burden of proof – beyond a reasonable doubt – being solely the prosecution's and went into an explanation about how jurors could believe all, part or none of any witness's testimony. He asked them to give the same kind of scrutiny to the nuns' testimony as they would any other witness. And then he peered at his watch.

"It's now 1:28," Egbert noted. "Twelve minutes since I told you the time was 1:16. A long, long time for Maurice diMontiferro to be standing with a weapon in his hand waiting. . . waiting. . . waiting for police to arrive and place him under arrest.

"You heard testimony about how Mr. diMontiferro had had previous convictions for assault, assault and battery, possession of a

201

dangerous weapon and assault and battery with a dangerous weapon. Judge Abernathy will instruct you that Mr. diMontiferro's criminal record was allowed into evidence for a limited purpose. You can't consider his court record as proof that he's a bad guy. When a defendant takes the witness stand to testify in his own defense, as my client has done here, you may only consider his criminal record as to how it applies to his credibility. I would suggest to you, in this particular case, Mr. diMontiferro's record should only help to convince you he is, indeed, credible. You heard how in each of the other instances, when my client was charged with a crime, he pled guilty to the charges against him. That should tell you one thing: When Mr. diMontiferro is guilty of a crime, he admits it; he owns up to it. But you also heard him vigorously deny the current charge against him. Because. . . he . . . didn't . . . do. . . it! Not this one. He doesn't plead guilty to something he didn't do!"

CHAPTER 32

HOW YOU GET A NUN TO TELL A LIE

Damn, Richie Egbert was good. Suddenly I could feel panic creeping back. It was kind of like a noose tightening around my neck.

"I'm reminded of the first case I tried in the Superior Court as an assistant district attorney," the prosecutor, Peter Constable, told jurors now that it was his turn to speak. That's the way it works in a criminal trial. The prosecutor gets the first word – he makes the first opening statement – and the last word in a criminal case. That's because the burden of proof is on the prosecutor. He has to convince jurors a defendant's guilt beyond a reasonable doubt.

"My first trial in the Superior Court was an armed robbery case and the defendant said he didn't do it. He couldn't have done it because he was out to eat with his brother and sister when the robbery took place. And then the defendant's brother and sister took the witness stand to support his alibi.

"The defense attorney in the case nearly apologized to jurors for putting the defendant's brother and sister on the witness stand to vouch for the fact that he was somewhere else when the crime occurred. The defense attorney told jurors that he would have preferred to put a couple of priests or a couple of nuns on the stand to say they were with his client. But it was the client's brother and sister he was with. That's who you generally spend your time with, your friends and your family. Yeah, if his client had known in advance he would be in need of an alibi, he would have gone to dinner with two priests or a couple of nuns. Because their word would be beyond reproach; people of the cloth wouldn't lie. A relative of the defendant, hey, you never know.

"So now you have two nuns telling you they were with Eva Green. And deep in your hearts you know that they wouldn't lie. And, oh, by the way, the defense attorney in that other case who longed for people of the cloth to vouch for his client, was Richard Egbert. 'A couple of nuns wouldn't lie,' Egbert told jurors in that case."

I couldn't help it. I only half listened to the rest of Peter Constable's closing. Richie Egbert had me totally panic stricken with his argument to the jurors. I wanted to hear Constable's response to Egbert's allegations about the 12-minutre delay. I thought that was pretty goddamn persuasive. And I didn't hear Peter theorize at all about what happened during those 12 minutes. Maybe he did offer some sort of explanation. Like I said, I wasn't really listening; I couldn't concentrate. Too shook up.

After I spent some time day dreaming . . . if that's what it was, day dreaming? It was more like day agonizing! I began listening to Peter Constable again and he was telling jurors that they shouldn't "give one iota of credence to the defense attorney's assertion that Mr. diMontiferro would plead guilty if he was, in fact, guilty."

"Yes, certainly, the defendant pled guilty in the past to crimes he had committed. It's called plea bargaining," Constable asserted. "By pleading guilty, Mr. diMontiferro got less of a penalty than he would have received had he gone to trial and was found guilty by a jury. And the crimes the defendant pled guilty to are penny-ante crimes compared to the charge he is now facing. Now, he's in the big time! Now, he's charged with a murder!

"Now, it's up to you. It's up to tell you to tell Mr. diMontiferro he's in the big time now. It's up to you to tell him there are no bargains!"

When Constable completed his argument and the judge was about to begin her charge to the jury, I hustled out of the courtroom. Hey, I had heard plenty of judges charge plenty of jurors about the law.

Besides, I was craving a cigarette. I went out the front door of the courthouse, sat on the concrete steps and lit my Marlboro. A moment later, Eva Green came out the door and sat beside me.

Per usual, it took me less than an instant to become deeply captivated by her dark, dangerous blue eyes.

"Cigarette?" I asked, holding out my box.

"I have my own," she said, producing a pack of Virginia Slims and extracting one.

I lit it for her.

"We probably shouldn't be seen here together," she suggested.

"Nobody's looking. We're the only ones here," I responded.

"How did you come up with those alibi witnesses?" I asked.

"You don't want to know." she said.

I took a deep drag off my butt.

"Actually, I think I do. Like you pointed out, there's no one here to eavesdrop."

"Do you remember the night I met you at *The Ambassador?*"

"How the hell could I forget that night? That was the night you lured me to the *Palace Hotel* to very rudely introduce me to diMontiferro, *The Incredible Hulk.*"

"Yeah, that's the night. I went to the telephone before we left. I told you I had a date that I was breaking. Well it was actually Maurice that I was calling."

"Yeah," I said, "I've since figured that out. You were calling him at the *Palace* to tell him we were on our way. The sucker – meaning me - fell for your phony pickup line and we *were* on our way."

She actually smiled now.

"Well, you made some kind of wiseass comment about how impressed you were that I'd break a date for you."

"There's no fool like an old fool," I responded.

"Oh, shut up, you're not old," Eva spat. "In any case, what did I tell you?"

Then she proceeded to answer the question herself.

"I told you not to be impressed, that I once broke a date with the same guy to go out with a couple of women. Well, that much was true. Maurice diMontiferro was once my boyfriend. And I broke a date with him to go out with Sister Agatha and Sister Therese."

"You're kidding!"

"Nope."

"And don't tell me you had sex with the sisters?"

Eva nodded proudly.

"A threesome," she said.

"And you threatened to blow the whistle on them if they didn't give you an alibi?"

"Exactly."

"I can't believe they fell for that threat. All they had to do was deny the whole thing. Who's going to take your word that it happened against two nuns saying it didn't.

Eva smiled.

Brilliantly.

"I've got pictures," she said.

"Of the three of you?"

She nodded.

Still smiling brilliantly.

"The three of you?

"Naked?

"Having sex?"

Again, she nodded.

"I'd like to see them sometime."

CHAPTER 33

JUST SPELL THE NAME RIGHT

I called into work on Wednesday and told whoever answered that I wasn't feeling nearly as bewitched as I had the day before, but I was still somewhat bothered and bewildered and felt that I should take another day before returning to the office.

After giving her instructions to the jury on Tuesday, Judge Abernathy released jurors for the day and told them that they could begin their deliberations fresh the next day. I had made up my mind that I would remain bothered and bewildered for as long as the jury was deliberating. This verdict was almost as important to me as the one when I stood accused of killing Lou Montgomery. I needed a guilty finding in this one. I needed the murder of Angelo "Angel" Macrillo to be put to bed. I guess the reason is pretty obvious.

There's an old courtroom axiom: A very quick verdict is definitely bad for the prosecution. Jurors don't want to give the appearance that they'll convict a defendant in a hurry. They always want to convey the impression that they're caring and sensitive and will examine the evidence carefully before dropping the hammer on the accused. They want to give the defendant the benefit of the doubt. Or, at least, they want to make it look like that way.

I've even heard it rumored that there've been juries that reached verdicts lickety-split, but held off announcing their decisions, just to make it look like they were doing their jobs.

Jurors began their deliberations somewhere in the vicinity of 10-o'clock Wednesday morning. About 10 minutes before noon, they announced that they had a verdict.

Damn.

An hour and 50 minutes? That had to be some kind of indoor record!

Nobody, but nobody, convicts in an hour and 50 minutes!

Another thing courtroom observers will tell you, is to pay attention to the jurors when they file into the jury box. If any of them are looking at the defendant, that's a sure sign that the verdict is not guilty. Jurors don't like to look into the face of a defendant they've just convicted.

I counted them. Hell, five of the jurors glanced at diMontiferro when they filed into the jury box. One, a hefty guy with an orange face who appeared to be sporting a blonde hairpiece, actually smiled. He was clad in a blue suit, white shirt and red tie; the tie hanging down somewhere in the vicinity of his crotch. He had one of those American flag pins attached to his lapel. The previous day, I also noted that the orange-faced juror had a tie hanging down to his crotch. Shit, you'd think someone would teach Juror Number 11 how to tie a tie.

"Madame forewoman, has the jury reached a verdict?" the clerk asked.

She responded affirmatively.

"On the indictment charging Maurice diMontiferro of murder in the first degree, how do you find?"

"Guilty."

"Fuck!"

The "Fuck!" coming from diMontiferro and directed toward the jurors.

He raised the defense table – which was no easy feat, it was large and made of what appeared to be heavy mahogany - and flipped it over in front of him.

He surged towards the jury box.

Richie Egbert ran him. diMontiferro grabbed him and tossed him pretty high into the air and Richie came crashing down on his rear end.

The first court officer to reach diMontiferro was swatted away like a troublesome mosquito.

I vaulted the railing that separates the onlookers from the participants in a trial and leaped onto *The Hulk's* back, my arms circling his neck. He continued toward the jury box, me riding piggy-back style. I circled my legs around the front of Maurice's and we went crashing to the floor.

We were quickly joined by three more court officers and two cops - the cops who had originally arrested diMontiferro. They had been at the courthouse throughout the brief trial. diMontiferro's arms were forced behind his back and cuffed. He was led to the courthouse's lockup - screaming and cursing.

The moment diMontiferro was pulled up to his feet, his eyes locked onto mine. I detected a deadly, violent note of recognition on his part.

Yes, his eyes were red.

Yes, they were wet.

But, fleetingly, he recognized me.

I wondered if, right then and there, he realized it wasn't only Eva Green; if he came to the startling conclusion, that there were at least two individuals who had very strong motives for Angel's life to come to an abrupt end.

I even wondered if he suddenly theorized that those two individuals acted in concert to make that happen.

If *The Incredible Hulk* had the opportunity to take the witness stand again, would he now point the finger not only at Eva Green, but would it land in my direction as well?

I wondered. . .

. . .Could he have deduced all of that when his eyes locked onto mine all so briefly at the courthouse?

Nah, no way in hell.

He never would have reached that conclusion.

He was very far from being the brightest bulb on the tree!

I'll tell you what; cigarettes certainly taste a hell of a lot better after a jury has returned a verdict and a big lug like Maurice diMontiferro has just taken the fall for a slaying you, yourself, committed. Standing on the white cement steps in front of the Providence courthouse I took a very deep drag on my Marlboro, breathing easily for the first time in months.

After a couple of minutes, I noticed a guy on the sidewalk looking at me. . . Juror Number 11. He meandered toward me, walked up the courthouse steps – his red tie hugging his crotch – and bummed a cigarette. Then he asked me for a light.

"Would you like me to smoke it for you, too?" I chided.

"Hell, no; I'll do that myself," he spat.

"You know, I noticed when the jury was entering the jury box, you looked at the defendant and flashed a big smile. At the time, I figured that had to be an indication that you had acquitted him. What the hell was that big grin all about."

"That was just my way of saying to the big, dumb lug: 'We got you, sucker! You're goin' away for a very long time!"

"Imagine him tryin' to blame that beautiful broad who used to be his girlfriend? Did you see her sittin' there in the courtroom? Goddamn beautiful, great eyes! And built like a brick shithouse; not a brick outta place!"

It was the first time I had ever heard anyone use that phrase except for Tony Lombardi and myself.

"What the heck did she ever see in him, the big lug?"

It was just about then that I saw her standing on the sidewalk. She took a small notebook out of her purse, jotted down something and ripped off the page.

Then she headed up the steps where Juror Number 11 and I were smoking. She handed me the slip of paper and headed back down the stairs.

"Hey, wait a minute," I protested, but Eva Green walked away as if she had never heard me.

I opened up the small slip of paper and read: "The Palace Hotel. 7 p.m."

"Wow! What does it say?" Juror Number 11, obviously impressed, asked.

"She wants to meet me tonight," I responded.

"You hot shit," he said as we simultaneously finished our butts. I walked over to an ashtray up against the building, crushed the butt and left it there. Juror Number 11 dropped his to the concrete step and crushed it with his shoe.

As Juror Number 11 began his descent down the stairs, he turned and called: "Hey, when you meet that broad tonight, give her a little squeeze for me, would ya?"

I didn't respond.

I lit another cigarette and was joined by Audacity who appeared at the doorway.

"You know how you asked me not to mention I saw you here at the trial? How you called in sick – or whatever it was you called in – and you didn't want it to get back to Beckerman that you were here?"

"Yeah."

"And I told you I wouldn't tell anyone I saw you here?

"Well, all bets are off. You're part of the story. Hell, you made yourself a major part of the story when you leaped over the railing and tackled diMontiferro."

"Yeah, OK, just do me a favor, would you, Audacity?"

"What's that?"

"Make sure you spell my name right."

CHAPTER 34

WE'VE ONLY JUST BEGUN

The night was magical. Eva Green was more beautiful than ever. Her eyes were the most beautiful in the world; deeper and darker than the deep blue sea, twice as deadly. But this particular night there was something more about them. There was a twinkle in them. One that I had never seen – or, at least, never noticed before.

Shit. . . maybe I was . . . falling . . . falling . . . in love.

"You're late," I said as she approached the table where I was seated in the *Palace Hotel* lounge.

"I'm sorry," she responded. "Punctuality isn't my strong suit."

I stood, gave her a kiss tenderly on the lips, went to the bar, got her a drink and returned to the table.

"You're very late," but then I quickly added, "but you can get away with being very late; you're also very beautiful."

From the jukebox:

We've only just begun to live
White lace and promises
A kiss for luck and we're on our way
We've only just begun.

Someone with a bunch of quarters was feeding the jukebox vigorously and flooding the lounge with the *We've Only Just Begun*" message from The Carpenters. It had played a couple of times before Eva arrived in the lounge and now continued after she joined me.

I was never much of a Carpenters' fan, but the message of this particular tune seemed appropriate at the moment and I got a little bit into it. I figured, yeah, maybe Eva and I had just begun. Now that Maurice "*The Incredible Hulk*" diMontiferro was convicted and was up the river where he belonged. Well, maybe he didn't belong there. But there he was – up the river – and now Eva and I didn't have to fear being seen together?

And so I asked: "How about it? Should I get a room upstairs? Are you planning on spending the night?"

Before the risin' sun we fly
So many roads to choose
And we'll start out walkin' and learn to run
And, yes, we've just begun.

"No, don't get a room. I want you to make an honest woman out of me before I give myself to you. Besides, it's Thursday; don't you have to go to work in the morning?"

"Yeah, I suppose I do."

"How about you, do you have to go to work in the morning?" I asked.

"I don't work any longer," she responded. "I'm independently wealthy."

She reached into her purse and pulled out a small box.

And handed it to me.

I opened it and you could have knocked me over with a feather.

A ring!

A diamond ring!

A man's diamond ring!

A stone as big as Gibralta!

The largest hunk of ice I had ever seen – or could possibly hope to see - in my life!

"Will you marry me?" she said.

"You've got to be kidding," I blurted.

"I've never been more serious in my life."

Sharing horizons that are new to us.
Watching the signs along the way
Talkin' it over just the two of us
Workin' together day by day
Together
Together.

"This can't be real, it can't be a real diamond," I gasped.

"Of course, it's real," she protested, "I'd never give you a stone that wasn't real."

"It must have cost you a fortune."

She paused, then added, "I told you, I'm independently wealthy."

"Where'd you get all your loot?"

"Angel," she said.

"Angel?"

"Yeah, after Angel bit the dust – and I thank you for that; I thank you for saving my life – I found his stash, a shoe box filled with bills. Very large denominations. It was certainly extremely thoughtful of Angel to put it away for me."

"How much?" I asked, "How much was in the stash?"

"Plenty, More than plenty. Well, I'll admit I spent a very big chunk of it on your ring. But there's more. A lot more. It will keep us living comfortably for a very long time."

And when the evening comes, we smile
We'll find a place where there's room to grow.
And, yes, we've just begun.

"You haven't answered my question," she noted.

And when I didn't respond right away, she added: "Will you marry me?

"What do I have to do, get down on one knee?" she asked.

Then I noticed her not looking at me, but beyond me. A very inquisitive look on her face.

"I saw someone looking at us through the glass door, but she's not there now."

I took a gulp of my vodka and tonic, wiped my mouth with the back of my hand and said, "No."

She looked crushed.

"No," she said, her voice now trembling. "You won't marry me?"

"No, you don't have to get down on a knee. Of course I'll marry you."

Her smile that followed was radiant.

She told me she'd meet me again the following night, Friday. We'd get a room upstairs and spend the night together then. But first, she said, we'd be married. Right there in the lounge of the Palace Hotel.

"Your friend, Andre, will perform the ceremony," Eva said. "You know, just like the captain of a ship.

"That's why I was so late meeting you. I was out front, talking to Andre. I convinced him he should perform the ceremony."

"Since when can a hotel owner perform a wedding ceremony?"

"Why not? It doesn't have to be legal. As long as you and I feel married. What does a wedding license or marriage certificate mean anyway? They're just pieces of paper. It's what's in our hearts that counts."

"And who's going to attend this ceremony?' I asked. "Are you inviting your folks, your mom and dad?

"My mom and dad are dead. Whoever is in the lounge at the time will be at the wedding. It will be a spectacular, spontaneous event for whoever is here!

"We'll spend the night – our wedding night – in a room upstairs. Andre said there's a room you've used before. It has a waterbed in it. He said that's the one you'd want. Said it will serve as a honeymoon suite."

"Yes, it will serve very nicely," I agreed.

"So, how about it, will you marry me?"

"I already said I would."

Eva leaned forward and gave me a deep, abiding kiss."

We've only just begun
White lace and promises
A kiss for luck and we're on our way
We've only just begun."
That's right; the Carpenters were filling the air once again.

CHAPTER 35

. . . RAINING HARD IN 'FRISCO

I sat at the same table at the *Palace Hotel* with a vodka and tonic the next night. There were two police cruisers outside the hotel when I arrived. Once inside, I learned there had been an armed robbery shortly before. The place was crawling with cops and excitement. From the jukebox we learned that "it was raining hard in 'Frisco." Harry Chapin, a cab driver in the melody, recalled a sentimental journey with his fare – a former girlfriend by the name of Sue – to 16 Parkside Lane. I guess The Carpenters fan wasn't in the lounge and commandeering the juke box this particular night.

Good thing. . . I much preferred Harry Chapin.

She took my breath away when the most beautiful chick this side of the Cape Cod Canal strolled in and sat down beside me.

Nope, not Eva Green.

It was Barbara looking more ravishing and beautiful than . . . than . . . well, more beautiful than I had ever seen her look before. And younger. You've got to remember, she was 15 years older than me, but she waltzed into *The Palace* lounge looking younger than springtime. What's that they say about not appreciating what you have until you lose it?

She was wearing the dress I always told her was my favorite. Probably chose that one to drive me more than a little bit crazy.

She sat down beside me and folded her arms in front of her, sort of hugging herself. Her tongue slowly made its way across her top lip. Something she did quite often. Very sexy. I think it was pretty much subconscious on her part, though.

She reached out, took my left hand into hers and said: "Nice ring."

After a slight hesitation; "Where'd you get it?"

Another slight hesitation, then: "Don't lie; I saw."

"Then there was no reason for you to ask," I responded, "and there's no reason for me to lie."

"I just wish it wasn't her," Barbara said. "I wouldn't feel nearly as bad if it were anybody but her."

"What do you mean? You don't know her!"

"I just wish like hell it wasn't with a girl you cheated with when we were together."

That threw me for a loop.

"What in God's name are you talking about?"

"The night you came home so late . . . well, one of the nights you came home so late. I was pretending to be sleeping when you came into the bedroom," she responded. "Minutes before, you were making out with the bitch. Making out with her in *your* car. The dome light on for all the world to see. I watched you from our living room window. You're sitting there making out, sitting in a spotlight! Like you were auditioning for a part on PEYTON PLACE. Then she drives off in *your* car."

We both fell silent for a minute.

Barbara's tongue whisked slowly – ever so slowly – across her bottom lip.

God, if she only knew what she did to me when she did that.

At some point, when we were sitting there, our hands just seemed to come together again. I don't think she consciously took my hand – and I know I didn't take hers – but our hands sort of came together. Loosely. She wasn't holding my hand and I wasn't holding hers, but our hands were touching and she kind of fingered the gigantic rock on my ring finger.

"What's that supposed to be, an engagement ring?" she asked.

"Something like that," I said.

"I'm surprised she didn't get down on one knee and ask you."

"I told her that she didn't have to."

Barbara didn't respond. I'm certain she didn't like hearing it. She stood and disappeared around the corner.

No "Goodbye!"

Or "I'm leaving."

She didn't say anything at all.

She just stood up and walked around that corner.

I waited a few moments and decided to get to my feet to make certain Barbara had exited the premises.

When I turned the corner, Barbara was leaving the ladies' room. She didn't notice me behind her.

Call it intuition or just an uneasy feeling.

If this were a movie, this is where we'd begin to hear some eerie, uneasy music.

I don't know if you believe me or not and I don't really care if you believe me or not – but I heard the music. I swear I heard the music.

I passed Andre's office, giving me a full view now of the lobby, the front desk and the front door. I saw Barbara by the front desk now and – damnit!– Eva was walking in the front door.

The music frantically building now.

Building. . .

Building. . .

Building. . .

Without hesitation Barbara grabbed a letter opener from the front desk counter.

She walked deliberately, steadily and boldly toward Eva.

. . . To a crescendo!

And Barbara plunged the letter opener into Eva's side.

221

One!

Two!

I don't know how many times!

Barbara dropped the letter opener onto the carpet and stood there.

Her mouth open.

A perplexed look on her face.

Just then Andre and a uniformed cop who had responded to the armed robbery came out of Andre's office.

The cop fumbled for his sidearm, telling Barbara she was under arrest, to stay exactly where she was.

Which she did.

When the cop's sidearm didn't come easily out of its holster, he gave up on that thought and, instead, reached for his handcuffs.

He slapped the cuffs on Barbara - her hands behind her back – and knelt to tend to Eva.

He checked her pulse.

"She's dead!"

He told Barbara she was under arrest and had a right to remain silent.

"You have a right to an attorney," the cop told Barbara. "If you can't afford an attorney, one will be provided for you."

The cop grabbed Barbara's arm and began leading her toward the front door.

"Barbara!" I shrieked. "Don't say a damn thing! Not a goddamn thing!"

Moments later – it seemed like a year –Detective Johnny McCracken had arrived on the scene to take over the investigation. McCracken and I had a history. Our perspective jobs would bring us together from time to time, he being a detective and me a newspaper reporter. But we really got to know each other when Johnny became a witness when I was charged with murder. At one point in the trial if Johnny had chosen to lie, he probably would have hung me. But he told the truth and I think that's when the scales of justice in the case began to tilt in my direction. I just may have owed my freedom to Johnny McCracken.

So now he was taking over the investigation into the stabbing death of Eva Green. There was a much younger, wide-eyed detective, next to him. Wearing thin gloves, Johnny placed the letter opener into an evidence bag.

I can't begin to tell you everything that was swirling through my head at the moment. Barbara, through the most grotesque action possible, had just shown me how much she actually loved me and how much I had hurt her. And I both loved and hated Barbara for it.

Who should pay for this crime? Certainly Barbara should, but hadn't I cruelly driven her to it? And, after all, didn't I deserve to be punished?

I took a few steps forward and I said, "Johnny."

McCracken flashed a very faint smile.

Just to register recognition.

"Rocky."

"Johnny, I gotta talk to you."

He gave me the slightest of nods.

"They got it wrong. The uniformed cops. They arrested Barbara Sovino. They got it wrong. I did it. I killed Eva."

"I don't think so," Johnny responded.

"Yeah, I did, I killed her."

"Really?"

The young, wide-eyed detective apparently didn't want to hear any of it. He sidled up to Johnny's side to present his case. He was telling Johnny that the assailant was obviously left handed because the letter opener was plunged – several times – into Eva's right side. The young investigator said he knew Barbara, knew her personally, and knew her to be left handed.

"And do you know the young man standing before us and telling us he did it?" McCracken, making no attempt to keep his voice down. "He's Rocky Scarpati. And, in case you've been living in a bubble, Rocky Scarpati was quite a prize fighter in his day and his bread and butter punch was a left hook. A LEFT hook."

Much to the young detective's dismay, Johnny McCracken, still gloved, reached into the evidence bag, which wasn't yet sealed, and retrieved the letter opener. McCracken's partner started to object, but Johnny tossed him a look that would have stopped Red "the Galloping Ghost" Grange in his tracks.

Johnny held out the opener toward my left hand and said: "Show me how you stabbed her."

"But" and that was all the young cop got out before Johnny barked, "Shut the fuck up!"

I took the opener Johnny had offered it to my left hand and slowly pantomimed three left hooks to the body.

"Three times?" McCracken said as if questioning.

I slowly showed him another left hook to the body in slow motion.

My eyes never leaving Johnny. Looking for any clue.

"Four times," McCracken said.

This time, Johnny said it with conviction, as if it were a statement.

"That's right, four times," I confirmed.

My good friend, Andre, was still at the doorway to office. Thankfully, goddamn thankfully, he picked up on what I was attempting to do.

"Detective McCracken," he said. "I saw the stabbing. Yeah, it was Rocky who did it. Not the woman they arrested."

Then a particularly good-looking chick behind the front counter spoke up. Taking the lead from her boss, she volunteered.

"I saw it, too." Nodding in my direction, she added, "it was him; not the woman."

"OK, Rocky, You're under arrest. You have the right to remain silent. . ."

And so on.

You know the drill.

CHAPTER 36

AS THE CLYDESDALES PRANCED...

A dozen Budweiser Clydesdales were prancing through my head the next morning as I sat in a basement cell at the Brockton District Court waiting to be arraigned. It was the worst hangover in the history of hangovers and I easily would have given my right arm – no questions asked – for a couple of Oxycodone. My mouth was dry, my head was bursting and I had the shakes. I felt like a leaf pretty near the top of an old oak tree being gently tossed around by the proverbial *breeze that seemed to whisper Louise.* Shit, there I was in all kinds of pain, sitting in a cell about to be arraigned on a charge of murder and here I am, sitting here now and talking to you about song lyrics!

A court officer I had known since my elementary-school days approached the cell and nodded. I suppose it should have been a rather awkward moment, you know, my being charged with murder and all, but it really wasn't. Not for me, anyway.

"Hello, Nick, how you doin'?" I asked.

He didn't respond.

I wasn't expecting him to.

Nick and I used to play sandlot baseball together. He wasn't very good. Always one of the last kids picked and generally sent out to a somewhat grassy knoll in right field to wile away the time when the other team was at bat.

Nobody hitting a thing to right field.

I was a much better ballplayer.

A born shortstop.

Nick handcuffed my hands. My legs were already shackled at the ankles. Nick's hand on my elbow, he led me out of the cell, into an elevator and eventually into the first-session courtroom.

I was guided to a small wooden box, smack-dab in the middle of the courtroom. A railing running away from the box, both to the right and the left, separated onlookers from trial participants.

Yeah, I was definitely the center of attention.

Something I would have appreciated under different circumstances.

I immediately glanced to my left and saw Audacity sitting in a jury box reserved for the press. A ball-point pen clenched in her hand. The slightest of smiles and she nodded in my direction. I returned the nod. There were several reporters from the Boston papers there and one from the Quincy Patriot-Ledger.

Word of my arrest got around. That was, after all, the reason for so many reporters. *The Examiner* was the only paper that covered the Brockton District Court on a daily basis.

Once again, I was very big news.

The Examiner photographer, Craig Mathers, must have had his camera set to speed dial. He was snapping away photos as I shuffled into the courtroom – the shuffling due to those damn shackles around my ankles. For the longest time, photographers weren't allowed in Massachusetts' courtrooms. Newspapers used to rely on artists to sketch likenesses in courtroom proceedings. But now one photographer was allowed into court proceedings and he – or she – was expected to send photos to any newspapers interested in a particular case.

And, as I said, Craig Mathers had the honor of being the "pool" photographer this particular day.

The clerk called my name.

My cue to stand.

"In the matter of the commonwealth versus Rocco Scarpati, you are charged with first-degree murder," the gray-haired gentleman – the most gentle of all gentle men - said, "how do you plead?"

"Guilty."

My plea resulted in an audible gasp from several individuals in the courtroom. You don't hear it all that often in District Court. And never on a charge of murder in the first degree.

Then, suddenly, from the rear of the courtroom, I heard, "No, Your Honor, that's not true at all!"

I knew the voice and reeled around to see Kevin Reddington, briefcase in hand, hustling inside. Like a knight in shining armor, aboard his trusty steed, rushing to the aid of a pretty young damsel in distress. Of course, Kevin was no knight and he was clad in suit and tie rather than shining armor. And, obviously, I was no damsel. And no way in hell was I in distress. I was handling the situation precisely the way I wanted it handled.

Sure, it was a split decision I had made the night before . . . to step forward and say it was I, Rocky Scarpati, who plunged the letter opener into Eva Green's side. Plunged it in four times. Due to Johnny McCracken's prompting.

"Well Attorney Reddington, so nice of you to join us," Judge Michael Carlyle remarked, putting emphasize on Kevin's tardiness. Carlyle was a wiry little guy with dark hair and dark-rimmed glasses that were too large for his face.

"Are you representing Mr. Scarpati?"

Kevin glanced in my direction to see if I had any apparent objection or anything at all to say about that and, when I didn't react, he responded, "Yes, Your Honor, and Mr. Scarpati can't plead guilty to the charge because, quite frankly, he's not guilty."

"OK, we'll enter a plea of not guilty on Mr. Scarpati's behalf and continue the case four weeks from today for status," Carlyle noted.

"And now, let's turn to the question of bail."

"The commonwealth would be seeking remand," Assistant District Attorney Antonio Esposito noted. "It's a murder case," he said, underlining the obvious.

Esposito, thin, blond hair and blue eyes, didn't look Italian. And he looked young enough to be in high school.

"Mr. Scarpati isn't a flight risk," Reddington said. "He isn't going anywhere. As I'm certain you're aware, Your Honor, not all that long ago, Mr. Scarpati faced a murder charge in Rhode Island. He made bail in that case and appeared each and every time the case was called.

"And, I might add, he was eventually found not guilty."

"The difference being – and it's a humdinger – that he's already told us here today, that he's guilty," Carlyle pointed out.

"He misspoke," Reddington shot back, not missing a beat.

"Hmm," was the only reaction he got from the judge.

"I'll set bail at $10,000 cash or $100,000 surety."

I made bail later that day. Folks were lined up in the clerk's office at the district courthouse, clamoring to put down $10,000 for my release. Lined up right down the corridor and out the door! Obviously they were fans of my Wednesday column on *The Examiner's* editorial page. If you believe that, I've got a bridge that spans the water from Brooklyn to Manhattan that I'd like to sell you.

But I *was* bailed out later that day. Reddington telephoned *The Examiner's* publisher, William J. Casey, about my predicament and William high-tailed it to the clerk's office to purchase my freedom.

When I reported for work Monday morning, the first thing I did was hop on over to William's office. When I walked into his office, this time we said it in unison, "What do you hear? What do you say?"

He smiled.

So did I.

"Remind me to instruct Marie not to allow self-confessed murderers to come barging into my office," Casey quipped.

Referring to William's description of me as a "self-confessed murderer," I noted, "so you read Audacity's story about my arraignment?"

"Of course I did," William responded. "I read the paper, front to back, on a daily basis."

That surprised me a little bit. I thought of a very well-known story that went around *The Examiner* about one of the editorial conferences the editors held on a daily basis. According to legend, Casey told the editors that he really wasn't much of a reader. He told them – almost bragging – that the only book he ever read was BLACK BEAUTY when he was a kid.

William said: "I hope you're not angry at Audacity for writing about your attempt to plead guilty to the murder charge. It happened; she had to report it!"

"Of course she did," I concurred. "Hey, don't forget, I'm a reporter, too. I've written a few stories about courtroom happenings. Of course I'm not angry at her. If she hadn't reported on my arraignment, I'd have chewed her ass off."

"From what I've heard," Casey quipped, "Audacity has an ass you wouldn't mind chewing."

"Where the hell did you hear that?" I wanted to know.

"Can't tell you," William replied. "You know a newspaperman can't reveal his sources."

"Hey, the reason I'm here, I just want to thank you – thank you from the bottom of my heart – for putting up my bail."

"I had to," he said, "I didn't want Wednesday to roll around without my star columnist's piece on the editorial page. I know there are a lot of people that look forward to your column on a regular basis and I didn't want to disappoint them."

My column on the editorial page was titled LIKE IT IS.

"It was a very wise decision you made by springing me from the lockup to write this week's column," I boasted. "It's going to be a real humdinger!

"This week's is going to win a New England Press Association award," I boasted.

"Hey, wait a minute, you're not going to . . .?

"Never mind, forget I asked."

CHAPTER 37
LOOKING . . . BEWILDERED AND PERPLEXED

"Are you out of your mind? I'm not going to allow you to use our editorial page to tell the world you're a murderer!"

Nope, it wasn't William Casey doing the ranting and raving after I turned in my column late Tuesday afternoon. It was Managing Editor Hugh Beckerman, a large, bulky, partially bald, red-faced man, getting redder by the moment. Blood vessels popped out of his head. His breath reeked of alcohol. I shouldn't say anything about that, however. My breath probably did, too. "It's not gonna run! I won't allow it! Get back to your typewriter and give me a column I can actually print."

I had gone into the office late Monday to write the column. That's when all my columns - due to be turned in Tuesday morning – were written.

"Not going to run?" I shot back. "It's great! I want to appeal! I want to hear from William Casey that it's not going to run!"

"It's not up to Casey whether the column runs or it doesn't run," Beckerman shot back. "That's what he pays me for. He pays me to make those decisions. Besides, he agrees with me!"

"He agrees with you? He read it . . . and he agrees with you!"

"That's what I said, didn't I?"

"Well, I want to hear it from the man himself!"

I turned on my heels and boldly headed for Casey's office. I wasn't as confident as I was pretending to be. Maybe William Casey read it and didn't like it. Or maybe he would back up his managing editor even if he did like the column.

Out of the corner of my eye as I turned away from Beckerman, I noticed him scooping a few sheets of copy paper from his desk and then coming after me. I assumed it was my column.

The one thing I had going for me, I figured, was the fact that William Casey and I had a pretty good relationship and, due to my conversation with him the previous day, he knew how important this particular column was to me.

As you've probably guessed by now: the column chronicled the events of Thursday, Oct. 31, 1976. Or at least what I wanted law enforcement officers, the court and the general public to believe happened at *The Palace Hotel* on Oct. 31, 1976. I opened the column by talking about meeting Barbara, my soul mate and love of my life in the lounge. How we had split one night months before after I beat the shit out of her in a jealous rage. But how – on this particular night – she had answered my dream and prayers and forgave me. We were going to move back in together and start our love affair anew.

Barbara (both in fact and in fiction) excused herself and got up to use the ladies' room. The music in my head began very low – very slow – and I had a haunting premonition that something catastrophic was about to take place. I got up from my chair, walked to the corridor and saw my darling pass the men's room, which is exactly what happened the dramatic night in question. Barbara entered the ladies' room, I noted in my column.

This is how my column described what happened next:

"Without really knowing why, I passed the ladies room and entered the lobby. The imagined music in my head was driving me there and then it reached a nerve-shattering and bone-crushing crescendo. Eva breezed through the front door as if she were floating on sunshine. I hurried toward her.

"Eva was going to tell Barbara, the love of my life, about our affair, Eva's and mine!

"As Eva Green approached, a slight smile on her face, the haunting music in my head ended abruptly. Replaced by an extremely deep, baritone voice. Sounded like James Earle Jones. Angry. An angry James Earle Jones, commanding me to 'Kill her!

'Kill her now!'

'Before she talks to Barbara!'

"Out of the corner of my eye. I spotted a letter opener on the front desk counter.

"'Kill her!' Jones repeated.

"I did . . .

". . .Grabbed the letter opener and approached the bitch who was threatening to ruin my life.

"And, the letter opener in my grasp, threw my patented, near legendary left hook.

"One.

"Two.

"Three.

"Four times."

"I dropped the letter opener.

"Staggered back.

"Slowly.

"To nowhere in particular.

"Barbara Sovino wandered back from the restroom and then rushed up to Eva Green's body – no apparent reason – and that's where she was when police arrived.

"They placed her under arrest. . . until my conscience got the better of me and I told Detective McCracken that it was, in fact, me and not Barbara who had delivered the fatal blows."

"Now I'll tell you the same thing I told McCracken that night. It was I, not Barbara Savino, who killed Eva Green. Rest assured, I killed Eva Green.

"I killed her in the name of love . . . in the name of my love for Barbara Sovino!"

When we reached the entry way to Beckerman's office, I asked his secretary to let him know we were there.

She pressed a button and when Casey responded over the intercom, she said: Hugh Beckerman and Rocky Scarpati are here to see you sir."

"I'm right in the middle of something, is it important?"

Beckerman immediately said it isn't important.

I followed him saying: "Yes it is, it's very important."

"Come on in," Casey said.

Once inside, almost without prelude, Beckerman shouted: "It can't run! We can't have one of our writers bragging about being a murderer. That's not journalism; it's trash! It's yellow journalism; it's tabloid trash!"

"Well, let me read it; I'll see if I agree," Casey said.

So he hadn't read the column as Beckerman had suggested earlier.

At that point, I looked over at Beckerman, certainly with daggers.

He didn't return my stare.

He didn't look at me at all. Not even a glance.

Knew he wouldn't.

Beckerman reached across the desk to hand William my column.

As he read, I searched William's face anxiously for a reaction.

Didn't get one.

Then, unbelievably, a smile.

"Sounded like James Earle Jones," he read out loud.

Moments later, William placed the copy paper onto his desk.

"Very well written," he said.

"But Beckerman is right. It doesn't belong on our editorial page."

A broad smile from the dude sitting beside me.

"It isn't a column or an opinion piece. It's hard news. Shocking! Captivating! Can't-put-it-down reading! It belongs on page one!"

"It most certainly does not!" Beckerman shot back, probably disagreeing with William Casey for the first time in his life.

Casey ignored his managing editor's objection.

"I'm going to instruct John Livingston to put it on Page One," Casey said. Then he looked at me, winked and added: "I'll tell him to give it a good play."

"It's a goddamn column," Beckerman said. "On page one, you want the column?" This was a near shout from Beckerman.

"I'll tell John to insert an editor's note on the top, telling people that this is Rocco Scarpati's LIKE IT IS column that normally runs on the editorial page, but because of its unique content, it running on page one today."

John Livingston was news editor at the paper. As news editor, his duties were generally to decide which stories would go on the front page and then to lay out the page – diagram which stories and photos go where. He was also probably my best friend at the paper. A particularly strong union man when he was in the union and still a friend of the union, in general, when he accepted the management post.

After our summit meeting in Casey's office, I returned to my desk to edit the stories that would appear on pages two, three and four and do the blueprint showing what goes where. Suddenly, out of nowhere and without warming, Stanley Beaumont, the *Examiner* photographer was beside me snapping pictures.

"Hey, you didn't give me a chance to smile," I said to him.

"This is going to run with your column. Due to the content, I'm sure you wouldn't want to be smiling," he responded.

That day, across the very top of page one, in big, bold letters – ALL CAPS - the headline screamed: 'I DID IT; I KILLED HER!'

Above the headline and underlined was the title of my column Like It Is:

Below the headline, my column and a picture of me looking a bit bewildered and quite perplexed.

CHAPTER 38
A LIGHT AT THE END OF THE TUNNEL

"Well, you certainly aren't making my job easy for me," Kevin Reddington quipped, his tie off and flipped onto his desk now that he was out of court for the day. It was the day after my blockbuster exploded over the top of page one of *The Examiner*. Kevin called the paper first thing in the morning and told me to meet him at his office after court at 4:30.

"Oh, yeah, and what job would that be, the job I'm making so difficult for you?" I asked.

"Getting a not guilty verdict of course; keeping you out of prison."

"I think that ship has sailed," I noted. "Besides I don't believe I belong out of prison."

"A lot of people who don't belong outside of prison, nonetheless, remain on city streets, outside of prison gates," Kevin retorted. "By the way, that was a very nice touch, the thing about hearing a voice, James Earle Jones, commanding you to kill the young lady. We might very well be able to translate that into a verdict of not guilty by reason of insanity. Temporary insanity!"

"You can't do that," I said.

"And why would that be?"

"Because you'd have to put me on the stand to say that I heard the voice."

"Ah ha. That wouldn't be a problem."

"Yes. . . it would. Because I'm standing here right now, telling you that the James Earle Jones thing – the voice telling me to kill Eva Green – never happened. That part of the column wasn't true; let's just call it journalistic license. And now that I've told you it didn't happen, you can't put me on the stand to say that it did because you'd be suborning perjury."

"You're right; no way in hell could I put you on the stand," Kevin agreed.

"Reading the police reports – and reading your column – there's also that question about the other young lady, Barbara . . . ah . . . Barbara."

"Sovino," I provided the last name.

"Yes, Barbara Sovino. The police report made it sound like the cops arriving on the scene thought it was Barbara Sovino who did the stabbing. Your column noted that she was next to the body when the police arrived. All of that could be woven into reasonable doubt."

"I wouldn't want that to happen," I said.

"And why is that? Do you have a major problem about being a free man?"

"No, but if I was acquitted because we introduced the theory that it was actually Barbara who did the murder, the authorities might actually believe the premise and go after her. I don't want that to happen. . .

". . . And, oh, by the way. . .

"She didn't do it, I did!"

"I expect the DA will be going to the grand jury any day now," Reddington noted. "Then you'll be arraigned in the Superior Court. You'll get your chance to plead guilty and make it count. A Superior Court judge can accept your guilty plea and sentence you.

"I think there's one thing you can let me do for you, though," Reddington allowed. "Let me talk to the assistant district attorney assigned to the case. Let me talk to him – or her – before your guilty plea. You'll, no doubt, be indicted on a charge of first-degree murder. That's life without parole.

"What you described in your column is really murder in the second degree. As you know from your days covering the courthouse, that's also a life sentence, but you'd be eligible for parole after 15 years. I shouldn't have too much of a problem convincing the prosecutor that you should be allowed to plead guilty to second-degree murder.

"Will you let me bargain the DA down to second degree murder . . . or are you intent upon serving the rest of your life behind bars?"

"Nope, certainly not," I responded. "I'd be perfectly willing to have you cut a bargain for second-degree. In fact, it would be very much appreciated. I'd like to see a light at the end of the tunnel."

All of this took place in Kevin's office, just off Belmont Street near the North Easton line. At precisely the same time, back in the center of Brockton, a slight, dark-haired man – his hair sprinkled with gray – sat at the bar in *The Mission* on Legion Parkway. He gulped a shot of whiskey, chased it down with a draft beer, winced severely, clutched his chest in front of him and keeled over to the floor, taking his barstool with him.

CHAPTER 39

WE KNEW THAT WOULD HAPPEN, DIDN'T WE?

I didn't hear about the whole tawdry, barroom affair until bright and early the next morning when I reported for work at *The Examiner* copy desk. News Editor John Livingston handed me printouts of the stories he wanted me to place on pages two, three and four and asked if I had heard about Jose Cervantes.

"What about Jose Cervantes?" I asked.

"He had a heart attack. He's dead."

"Cervantes' widow should sue the hell out of Blake Richardson and *The Examiner*," I said. "I told Blake Richardson that was gonna happen if he left Jose out on the road. I told him Jose would have a heart attack and kick the bucket. His wife should sue Richardson and *The Examiner* for everything they've got. We should be working for her this time next year."

"She might have a problem doing that," John Livingston responded.

"Oh, yeah, why?" I asked, "I told Richardson it was gonna happen."

"Because Jose had the heart attack at *The Mission* over a beer and a shot. During working hours. His *Examiner* truck parked out in front of the barroom."

"Shit!"

That's all I had to say about that.

"Shit!"

Shortly after the first edition of *The Examiner* was put to bed, I got a call from Blake Richardson. He said he'd like to talk; did I have a few minutes I could give him?

"Sure, I'll be down in five minutes," I responded.

I knew what was on Richardson's mind. He knew I'd be steaming about Cervantes and probably expected me to unload on him with both barrels. Then he'd fire back the thing about Jose hitting *The Mission* during working hours and imagined it was probably an alcohol-induced heart attack! The truck was out in front of the watering hole and Jose was probably going to drive it under the influence!

"Come on in," Richardson shouted when I rapped on his office door.

"What's new?" he said, baiting me, baiting me, waiting for my attack.

"Not much," I responded, refusing to take the bait.

"Did you know that Bill Conley got busted the other night for drunk driving?" Richardson asked.

I could understand how that may have created a baffling predicament for Richardson.

I knew Richardson and Conley were very good friends. Very likely best friends.

Conley wouldn't be able to fulfill his duties as a district manager if he couldn't drive a truck.

And certainly Richardson wouldn't want to be firing Bill Conley.

"I'm going to bring Conley into the shipping room. Have him work there."

"I think you're doing the right thing. Obviously, Bill's going to lose his license for a period of time. You're doing the right thing by moving him into the shipping room."

I headed for the door. Richardson could see his chance to come down on me about Jose Cervantes slipping away, so he hurriedly asked: "Rocky, did you hear about Jose Cervantes?"

Smiling, I responded: "Yes, Blake, I did; but we both knew that was gonna happen, didn't we?"

And I skipped out the door before he had a chance to respond.

CHAPTER 40
SOBER AS A JUDGE

Audacity gave me a little tidbit as soon as she returned from the Superior Courthouse. She said she'd be certain to spell my name right. Once again, I was big news. She said I'd be arraigned Monday.

Wonderful news.

One last weekend to spend with my loved ones.

Except I didn't appear to have any loved ones.

And, under the circumstances, I didn't think the timing was right to see Barbara.

Thrn, there was my daughter. Can't forget my daughter, Annie. She was just a toddler. Three? Three years old? I didn't even know for sure. Stop snickering, I never claimed to be a candidate for father of the year. But, right now, I figured maybe I should try to spend my last couple of days as a free man with Annie. But when I got back to my desk and called Annie's mom, Susan, to arrange it, Susan gave me some half-baked reason why that would be impossible. Susan was straight up to form, always making it difficult for me to see Annie.

So I spent most of the weekend drinking here and there and generally feeling sorry for myself. I was a pretty heavy drinker. And that's one of the things that scared me the most about going to prison. I would have one helluva time quitting the booze cold turkey. Shit, every afternoon I started to get the shakes about the time I got off work. Or shortly before. I wondered if that meant full-fledged DTs were right around the corner.

"Delirium is a disease of the night."

That's from THE LOST WEEKEND by Charles Jackson.

I used to tell myself not to worry about the dreaded DT's. Delirium tremors occur when you're off the booze. Just keep drinking; don't stay away from alcohol long enough for that to happen. I was really smug about the whole possibility.

Now, facing prison. I wasn't such a smart ass! Now I was worried.

So, before leaving for the courthouse Monday morning, I armed myself with four shots of vodka and chased them down with a beer. I figured that might put off the shakes for as long as possible, anyway. I wouldn't be standing there in the courthouse doing my version of shake, rattle and roll.

So I went to the Brockton Superior Courthouse feeling kind of light-headed, kind of woozy and kind of drunk. Kevin Reddington, my attorney, asked if I had been drinking. I guess it showed. A little bit, anyway. I told him no.

"If you've been drinking, you know, if you're drunk, the judge won't be able to accept your plea," Kevin warned.

"I'm going to be meeting with the assistant district attorney before your arraignment," Kevin said. "Hopefully, I'll come out of it with good news, You are prepared to go to prison today if they allow you to plead to second degree murder, aren't you?"

"I'm ready to go to prison no matter what they say. If they insist on first-degree murder, I'll plead to that."

"No, you won't," Reddington insisted. "What you described was a second-degree murder, a killing with malice aforethought, no pre-meditation. I won't let you plead to murder in the first degree."

I don't know exactly how I responded to that. I don't think I did.

Reddington came out of his meeting!

Good news!

The prosecutor was going to *let me* plead to murder in the second degree!

I'd be eligible for parole in 15 years!

Yup, great news. I hope you caught the sarcasm in my voice.

Today, I'd be going to jail.

Directly to jail!

No passing GO!

No collecting $200!

I was due to appear in the Superior Courthouse in front of Judge Augustus F. Wagner Jr.

When my case was called, I stood at the railway, my attorney by my side.

"Well, Mr. Scarpati, it's good to see you. Not under these circumstances, but it's good to see you."

"Good to see you also, Your Honor."

"I understand there's been an agreement for you to plead guilty to murder in the second degree."

"That's correct."

He then asked me a series of questions formulated to determine if I knew what I was doing and if it was of my own free will. If I knew that I had the right to go to trial and, if I did, the state would be required to prove my guilt beyond a reasonable doubt.

Yeah, I knew.

Gus instructed me to tell him what happened.

I'm not going to make you sit through that again. I told him the version with me killing Eva – not Barbara doing the dastardly deed. And I didn't tell him anything about the music, which I actually heard, or a voice telling me to do it, which you know I never heard.

When I had finished speaking, I guess Gus Wagner picked up on the same thing Kevin Reddington had earlier.

"Have you been drinking, Mr. Scarpati?" Wagner asked.

"No, Your Honor, I'm sober as a judge."

That got a few chuckles throughout the courtroom.

But none from the bench.

When they led me from the courtroom, I quickly scanned the spectators. I think I was hoping to spot Barbara.

I didn't.

But I was shocked to shit when I spotted Fredrica - Ricki. In all her glory, she was decked out in a wide brimmed hat, a colorful scarf and Jackie Kennedy sunglasses. The woman had class.

All her own.

But I didn't know what she was doing that day.

Witnessing my departure?

CHAPTER 41
IT IS A FAR, FAR BETTER THING THAT I DO...

When I met my cellmate later that day, it probably would have confirmed the worst fears of many a young man walking into the slammer.

He was the size of a garage. He had wide violent eyes, an outrageously nasty scar under the left one and his skin was the color of midnight in the desert. Darker than coal. And it shined. In spots, it seemed to have a bluish tinge. He was a gruesome, intimidating character, indeed. But, the moment he opened his mouth, any feeling of fear or intimidation on my part flew out between the steel bars. His voice was gentle and wispy. Kind of breathy. No dude with that sort of voice could pose any kind of threat.

However, I was in the cell about a half an hour before I ever heard his voice.

After he eyed me up and down and all around – and I did the same to him – he finally said in his falsetto tone: "My name is Bond."

"Bond?" I asked.

"Bond," he repeated.

"James Bond?" I asked.

It went right over his head.

"No, Harry," he said. "My name is Harry Bond."

By late afternoon, I was already getting the shakes. Pretty heavily. The thought of getting full-fledged DTs right there in the prison cell scared me. The shakes were one thing. But I had never had the DTs. But now I feared, I truly feared; that they were right around the corner. I was in a prison cell and no alcohol was in my reach.

I told the guard that I needed to go to the infirmary.

"Oh yeah, and why would that be?"

"Because I need a drink. I'm an alcoholic. I'm afraid I'd going to get awfully sick."

"You're on the wagon now, asshole," was the guard's response.

Nice guy.

I figured they should send the dude for sensitivity training.

I told myself that if I got the DTs bad enough, they'd send me to the infirmary.

Only, to be perfectly honest, I didn't want to experience them "bad enough."

I didn't want to experience them at all.

So I immediately came up with this plan: I was an actor. At least, I was once an aspiring actor. Hell, I was a theatrical-school dropout. This was my plan: I'd fake getting the DTs and make such a pain in the ass of myself that they'd put me on an express train to the infirmary where they'd give me meds to calm me down. I'd get the meds before the real-deal DTs actually struck me.

Hell, I could fake the DTs. I had read THE LOST WEEKEND. I had even seen the movie. If Ray Milland could give such a convincing performance of a dude suffering from alcohol withdrawal, I could, too. I was every bit the actor as Ray Milland.

"Delirium is a disease of the night."

I had no idea what time it was. I had the shakes now without faking them. For starters, I imagined tiny insects walking across the floor toward me. I saw them reach me. Begin to crawl on me.

I swatted the first few. But there were too many. I couldn't keep up. They crawled up me. Inside my dungaree legs. Going higher. I moaned. I swatted. Moaned louder. Swatted harder.

The insects were everywhere. All over me; all over the floor. The walls. They were everywhere.

"Keep it the fuck down, wouldya!?!" someone yelled.

Suddenly, I noticed a hole high on the wall of the prison cell. And the head of a mouse appeared. The cutest goddamn mouse you ever did see.

Just like the one Ray Milland saw in THE LOST WEEKED.

Then out of nowhere, an ugly, vicious predator.

A bat!

Attacking the mouse!

I saw it!

I believed it!

Hey, I was good!

I screamed!

I screeched!

The bat's fangs, its beak, penetrating the little mouse!

I screamed!

Again and again!

The little guy's blood dripped down the wall.

"Hey shut the fuck up in there! I'm trying to sleep!"

Delirium is a disease of the night.

Finally a guard arrived.

Took me to the infirmary.

Where I was shot up with medication.

And slept.

Peacefully.

They told me it would be three days before all the alcohol left my system. Anything I felt after that would be psychological, not physical. No delirium after that. Only in my mind.

I was returned to my cell after three days in the infirmary.

The very same cell.

Harry stared at me for the longest time.

Finally, he asked: "What your name?"

Trying to be funny, I responded.

"Bond, James Bond."

Phew!

Right over his head.

Again.

"Wow, my name is Bond," he said, "They must assign us cells by alphabetical order."

As I sat in my cell that first morning back from the infirmary, I was at greater peace with myself than I had ever been in my life. I was here, after all, doing time . . . time that definitely belonged to Barbara.

I probably should have hated Barbara. She had killed the woman I wanted to spend the rest of my life with. And I did hate Barbara for that. I hated her, could never forgive her.

But why did she do it?

She did it because she loved me too much.

And because she loved me so much; I loved her.

I suppose I could have been bullshit because I was sitting there behind bars for a murder I didn't commit.

But somehow I attributed that to poetic justice.

I had gotten away with shit before.

I probably belonged in prison before.

So it was karma.

I had it coming.

But I was doing it for her.

For Barbara.

It was a far, far better thing that I do, than I have ever done."

That was Dickens.

CHAPTER 42

IT IS A FAR, FAR BETTER REST THAT SHE GOES TO...

While I was sitting there feeling so goddamn good about myself, a guard appeared and told me I had a visitor.

It kind of surprised me.

It surprised me even more when I entered a tiny room, sat down in front of a pane of glass and saw Johnny McCracken, eye patch and all, sitting on the opposite side of the glass.

I picked up the telephone on my side of the glass and Johnny picked up his. Johnny whose testimony had helped me beat one murder rap and, of course, his actions at the Eva Green murder scene, helped me to keep Barbara out of the slammer.

"I've got some terrible news," Johnny said into the phone.

"It's Barbara.

"Her body was found in her apartment this morning.

"I'm terribly sorry, Rocky.

"She's dead."

I couldn't believe what I was hearing.

"Drug overdose."

ACKNOWLEDGEMENTS

Now that you've read NOBODY LIKES A FALLEN ANGEL, please take a few minutes and write a review about it on Amazon.com. It will be tremendously appreciated.

Right now, I want to thank my business manager and copy editor, Ronni, who also just happens to be my ever-loving wife, for all her work dealing with my publisher and editing the manuscript. I'll also give her a nod for keeping me alive through all kinds of life-threatening illnesses that have come my way from time to time. Without Ronni, they'd be no Angel, neither fallen nor flying high!

Thanks also to my son, Tom, chief of the Appellate Division of the Northwestern Massachusetts DA's office. Tom guided me through the legal aspects of the original Rocky Scarpati novel, NOBODY LIKES A FAT JOCKEY as well as the FALLEN ANGEL crime saga. I'm sending my love and appreciation to Tom as well as my daughter, Dawn; my other son, Bob, and my step-daughters, Lee and Jami.

While all of the events and most of the characters in ANGEL are purely fictional, a few real people were woven into the plot.

On several occasions Rocky Scarpati quoted his good friend – and mine, Tony Lombardi – now deceased.

Crackerjack attorney Kevin Reddington, restaurant owner Hank Tartaglia and Judge Augustus F. Wagner, were all good friends of Rocky in the book and all good friends of mine in real life.

Another crackerjack attorney Richie Egbert, now deceased, was also a real person

And Ricki Wahl, the flamboyant blonde Rocky meets on Nantasket Avenue in Hull, is the real deal.

Any similarities between any events or other characters in the book aet purely coincidental.

CPSIA information can be obtained
at www.ICGtesting.com
Printed in the USA
BVHW032032020421
604013BV00001B/9